Raphael Brous was born in Melbourne in 1982. He has studied law and neuroscience at Monash University. He currently plays music in the band Teenage Mothers and is a volunteer campaign director at the animal rights organisation Animal Liberation. He also appears on ABC Radio National with John Safran, debating matters of religion and animal rights. Currently based in Melbourne, Raphael has lived in London and Brooklyn. His recreation consists of skateboarding and obsessively reading.

I Am Max Lamm

Raphael Brous

corsair

Constable & Robinson Ltd
55–56 Russell Square
London WC1B 4HP
www.constablerobinson.com

First published in Australia by University of Queensland Press, 2011

First published in the UK by Corsair,
an imprint of Constable & Robinson Ltd, 2013

A copy of the British Library Cataloguing in
Publication data is available from the British Library

ISBN: 978-1-47210-597-4 (paperback)
ISBN: 978-1-47210-613-1 (ebook)

Typeset by TW Typesetting, Plymouth, Devon

Printed and bound in the UK

1 3 5 7 9 10 8 6 4 2

To my grandmothers, Hilda Brous and Olga Brooke

What shall I testify for you? What shall I compare to you,
O daughter of Jerusalem . . . For your ruin is as vast as the sea!
Who can heal you?

The Book of Eichah
(Lamentations)

ONE

Thursday 7 April, 2005

Twenty-four hours after Malik Massawi collapsed beneath a bus shelter, his murderer remained unidentified. They said the culprit was a skinhead thug from an Aryan supremacist gang. Or an Islamic extremist, deliberately provoking the riots by attacking a Pakistani teenager who had strayed from the fundamentalist Wahhabi creed. Or most likely (but seldom printed for reasons of newspaper circulation), the murderer was a petty crim, another junkie prowling Camden for enough coins to buy a teaspoonful of crack wrapped in cooking foil. Despite its bipartisan condemnation in the House of Commons, the teenager's murder was probably a bungled mugging, one of hundreds monthly in the capital.

No matter the facts, London's anger spread like a virus. Outrage breached the city's borders of £14 entrees and Mercedes SUVs parked ten minutes' walk from the drug dens of Dalston and Hackney's Murder Mile. The riots broke the capital's stoicism, cracking the resilience long hardened by the Blitz, the IRA's bombings, the Brixton riots, Princess Di's death and the 9/11 attacks.

Can you believe it? Strangers asked each other on the Tube, the bus, at the hairdresser's, in the queue at Tesco.

See the smoke from the burning shops in the East End?

See the boy's poor mother crying on the news?

It's the skinheads from the BNP that started it . . . It's the Pakis, they should go back to Currystan . . . It's the liar Blair and his fucking war . . . It's the bloody police. They attacked the protesters and made it worse! . . .

It's a shame the boy's dead.

They were frightened too. Much too dangerous on the night buses, they agreed in beauty salons, supermarket queues, doctors' waiting rooms, laundrettes. Mothers phoned their teenagers: *Where are you? Get home before the curfew!* Thousands of wary parents prevented their teenage Mahmouds, Zhangs, Indras, Imrans and Yaakovs from walking the night-time streets where a racist slayer apparently lurked. The fear, the chronic collective nausea, cut especially deep because Max Lamm bludgeoned the Pakistani teenager four months *before* the Tube suicide bombings of July 2005, four months before a terrorist cell from Leeds finally disintegrated the assumption vital to a city's calm – the assumption of safety during one's daily routines – thereby testing London's nerves just as terror had already shattered the vestige of sanctuary in Madrid, Manhattan, Tel Aviv or Baghdad. Nobody in a metropolis can be unimpeachably safe, yet until the Tube bombings many Londoners assumed otherwise.

Malik Massawi died of his injuries, the news hit the airwaves and the Bethnal Green riots commenced, stunning the nation's newspaper editors, pinstriped commentators and superannuated MPs, who had presumed that in the New Europe, this sort of messy, dangerous racial tension was restricted to the North African immigrant quarters of Marseilles or Amsterdam and hadn't listened to the

2

English working poor telling them otherwise. For months afterwards, at boardroom lunches in the city and dinner parties of Notting Hill, Malik Massawi's bloody spectre was inescapable. These horrid riots, the diners concurred over their antipasto, revealed that a slimy arcadia of xenophobia, strongly resurgent across the Channel, had propagated like a bacteria at home despite London's fondness for Brick Lane's vindaloo.

Max Lamm's unintended crime would not be forgotten. Not when the BBC news bulletins commenced with Malik Massawi's mother Priya, swathed in a black hijab, collapsing into her sister's arms outside the Central London Morgue moments after identifying her son's corpse. Not when, following the riot, armed constables patrolled Bethnal Green's shopping centre to deter nocturnal looters, or when the PM's press conference attracted nearly as many TV viewers as a World Cup qualifier. Not when hundreds of schoolchildren left half a tonne of flowers beneath the dead teenager's locker at the South Camden Community School and at the Walthamstow football club where he played goalie for the under 16s. Not when that weekend, most of the priests, reverends, rabbis and imams in London sermonised against the inhuman bigotry that, they presumed, had given the killer a reason to kill and the mobs a reason to destroy. And not when the boy's Leyton funeral, the Saturday morning thirty-six hours after his death, attracted a procession stretching two kilometres. Four thousand mourners, the newspapers reported, including, photogenically at the head of the throng alongside the victim's family, the prime minister in a black suit, head bowed, shadowed by fifteen bodyguards.

Unlike most crimes heinous enough for the front page, this one wouldn't disappear to exclusively haunt its victims. All Britain, not just her Asian and Middle Eastern communities, mourned Malik Massawi, a son of Pakistani immigrants whom the Associated Press eulogized as a devoted older brother to his sisters Mufasa and Dila, as a passionate Tottenham Hotspur fan and talented goalkeeper who, his father admitted, mixed with a bad crowd on their council estate, smoked pot and often skipped school, but would surely have blossomed through adolescence. The night that he never woke up, Malik Massawi was fifteen years old; who could deny that this underachieving student might have outgrown his adolescent rebelliousness and ultimately made it to university or even the professional football pitch? The memorials to this wayward teenager with arresting hazel eyes, a mop of black curls and an easy gap-toothed smile occupied more newsprint than the obituaries for many distinguished statesmen, scientists and writers.

But in the weeks following the riots, nobody writing the op-eds – not human rights lawyers hawking their positivist pluralism in the *Guardian*, nor thinktank wonks spruiking al-Qaedaphobia in the *Daily Telegraph*, nor even the mayor pleading for communal calm – nobody *really* knew what happened that fatal night in Camden.

The statement of multifaith conciliation co-authored by the Archbishop of Canterbury, the Chief Imam of Great Britain and the Chief Rabbi of the Commonwealth, published in the London papers the Sunday following the riot, was, of course, intriguing to the culprit. Flattering, the way John Hinckley Jr felt flattered after he shot President

Reagan and Jodie Foster appeared on TV to discuss her nutcase stalker-assassin. But in their public statements, all the bishops, rabbis, imams, these lauded, learned, bearded men, were wrong! Wrong about the '*deliberate racist attack against an innocent boy of Pakistani heritage*'. Wrong, so damn wrong that Max Lamm, in his oily subterranean hideout, couldn't help protesting aloud.

'You presumptuous fuckers! It was an *accident!*'

In a hole at 9.07 p.m., yelling at the newspaper, risking revealing himself to police if they were, at that moment, inspecting Hyde Park's most neglected grove.

For a day since accidentally killing the Pakistani teenager whose eulogies dominated the front pages of London's tabloids and broadsheets alike, Lamm had been hiding hungrily, filthily, in the capital's closest approximation to Dante's inferno. His purgatory – smeared in sausage fat, charcoal dust, petrified kebab skewers – was the maintenance hole beneath a barbeque in Hyde Park. A gas barbeque set into a rectangular counter of limestone, built thirty years before a nearby McDonald's reduced its use to once or twice a year. Underneath was the gap, long and deep enough for a vagrant to lie flat, between gas pipes and a sooty brick floor.

Some homeless bum had already slept down there, leaving a legacy of mouldy napkins, six-month-old newspapers, soured milk cartons, a crack pipe fashioned from kitchen foil, three disintegrating socks and a condom creased with dried semen. Lamm removed the trash upon discovering the hideout at 5.23 a.m. (the time he sharply recalled, the way his luminous watch blurred in the Hyde Park fog).

TWO

A murder. Reported in the London newspapers as the unwitnessed bashing of a fifteen-year-old Pakistani boy, beneath a bus shelter at Mornington Crescent, Camden Town, at approximately 4.18 a.m. on Thursday 7 April, 2005. The victim, Malik Massawi of Chalk Farm Estate, was a ninth-form student at the South Camden Community School on Charrington Street, Camden. A secondary college, among North London's most disadvantaged, where English is the second language learnt by almost eighty per cent of its students. Malik Massawi's corpse hadn't hit the autopsy slab before he made the BBC news bulletin at 10 a.m. Five hours later, the riots. In the Muslim quarter of Bethnal Green, about three hundred residents – Pakistani, Bangladeshi, a few dozen Afghanis – gathered outside their local MP's office to condemn the apparently racist murder. The rally was hastily organized by five Pakistani teenagers, including three of the victim's cousins. They carried spray-painted placards proclaiming in English, Urdu and Pashto: *Stop Hate Crimes Now!* or *Justice for Malik Massawi!* By the morning's end, hundreds of thousands of British Muslims knew about the rally through text messages, emails or news reports, and from 2 p.m. until 6 the crowd swelled to almost eight hundred people.

By three o'clock, the Metropolitan Police had cordoned off the pavement for TV crews. At four o'clock sharp, a contingent of forty-seven skinheads, many representing the British National Party; marched in to commence their counter-protest. Mostly they were pale twentysomething men wearing steel-capped boots, polo shirts buttoned to the neck, bomber jackets, crew-cuts. Their jackets bore the insignia of Combat 18, an openly neo-Nazi paramilitary organization founded as stewards for volatile BNP rallies. The outlines of iron bars were discernible beneath some of the men's shirts.

The skinheads unfurled banners advocating a moratorium on immigration, chanting in a baritone that would have prickled goosebumps at the Nuremberg rallies. '*Asia for Asians, Britain for Brits*' these heavyset men bellowed unwaveringly. '*Keep up the fight, keep Britain white!*' Amid the volley of rocks, bottles, drink cans and abuse in six subcontinental languages, thirty police separated the BNP gang from eight hundred furious Muslims and Hindus. The TV crews jostled for a clear view, however long the photogenic brawl would take to break out. Twenty minutes later, another chorus joined the cacophony: seventeen protestors from the Socialist Worker's club at University College (their entire membership save for two who were tutoring in the philosophy department that afternoon). With some carrying bookbags, the students unfurled a faded, tattered banner proclaiming *Nazi Punks Fuck Off* painted above a swastika bisected by a red line.

Had this rally occurred at night, the horde of flashing cameras would have outshone the streetlights. The photographers were especially fond of a nine-year-old Pakistani girl wearing a blue hijab, white stockings and a floral smock to her ankles. She stood at the police line, staring imploringly into a thug's lantern-jawed face and screaming in high-pitched Urdu. Nearby, a few skinheads talked into mobile phones, telling their wives or bosses that they were ill and off the job this afternoon.

Finally, the show commenced. Someone pitched two glass bottles at the police, striking a constable in the chest, and the violence erupted during a baton charge by officers who had never faced such a volatile throng outside a football pitch. The police line breached, a hundred Pakistani and Afghani men charged at their xenophobic provocateurs. A gang of local hoodlums joined in the fun, yelling numerous permutations of *fucking Paki terrorists* at the conspicuously devout protestors in beards or burqas.

Within a minute, anything at hand was a weapon: placards, umbrellas, rocks, glass bottles, drink cans, rubbish bins, steel poles pilfered from the flimsy barricade. Dozens of windows smashed, three police cars pelted with stones, a BBC news van damaged beyond repair and two picket fences torn apart to yield makeshift batons, as sixty police, armed with truncheons, tasers and pepper spray, couldn't contain the violence.

Fifteen minutes later, five police vans were stuck at the intersection of Patriot Square, four blocks from the riot's epicentre, as a thousand locals – chanting in Arabic, Urdu, Pashto, Farsi and English – took to the streets. At the head of the rally, the dead boy's cousins led the thunderous chorus . . . *Racist Murder! Racist Blair! Racist Murder! Racist Blair!* The skinheads, and the local hoodlums who had tripled in number, replied with their fists, boots and palings broken from the picket fence. But amongst the many, many images of the riots headlining the news bulletins that night, the most talked-about footage worldwide – appearing on every major TV network from San Francisco to Sydney to Santiago – wasn't the Bangladeshi children staring gape-mouthed at their fathers battering a police car with steel poles, nor an elderly Irish shopkeeper, his off-licence looted, defiantly scolding three white teenage thieves like the lone activist confronting a tank in Tiananmen Square. No, the most-broadcast footage of the 2005 East End riot featured an ITV reporter – wearing an absurdly nice Saville Row suit, wielding his microphone like a dapper Robert Capa at the D-Day landings – getting knocked out cold by a flying milk bottle as he solemnly intoned 'Who would have thought this could happen in Londo—'

At his press conference, the mayor condemned London's worst race riot since the Brixton uprising of April 1981. Nine policemen and twenty-three protestors were hospitalized, including a Bangladeshi engineering student bashed into a coma and a British–Iranian teenager critically injured by a brick thrown at his head. A Scottish bystander suffered spinal injuries from being trampled beneath a barricade; her physicians suspected that paraplegia would result. Dozens of storefronts were smashed, with three electrical retailers, a Nike outlet, an off-licence and a mobile phone dealership looted amid the chaos.

That night in Tower Hamlets, three Pakistani shops were firebombed by vigilantes who scrawled racist graffiti on the walls. A Bangladeshi social club was burnt down; on the front pages, its smoking ruins appeared like the charred exoskeleton of a monstrous alloy spider. Near Brick Lane, five turbaned Sikh teenagers were attacked by a mob of white youths. For the next forty-eight hours, police patrolled the East End from horseback and riot vans, enforcing the curfew from dusk. The damage bill exceeded £20 million and the glass-strewn streets, littered by torn cardboard packaging from looted stereos and TVs, attracted journalists in hordes unrivalled in London until the Tube bombings four months later.

For the remainder of that week at the Finsbury Park mosque, afternoon prayers overflowed not only through piety, but because hundreds of young men (and a few undercover police and investigative journalists) crammed in for the sermon by Abu Hamza al-Masri, known in the tabloids as 'The Hook'. Hamza the Egyptian-born imam who disfigured his face and lost both forearms in an explosion in Afghanistan, who delighted in looking monstrous with a milky shattered eye and two steel hooks for hands. At his pulpit, Hamza accused the prime minister of ordering the murder of a Muslim teenager in order to provoke the riot, demonize British-Muslims and win support for the unpopular alliance with Washington. Captivatingly employing the Arabic-English vernacular of the immigrant street, the handless preacher repeated his notorious sermon that was burnt onto CDs, sold at mosques from London to Leeds, and reprinted in the February 2008 issue of *Vanity Fair*.

'My dear brothers, if you can go, then go! If you can't go, sponsor! If you can't sponsor, speak! If you can't do all of this, do all of that! If you can send your children, send them! You must have a stand – with your heart, with your tongue, with your money, with your hand, with your sword, with your Kalashnikov! . . . Just do it! If it is killing, do it! If it is paying, pay! If it is ambushing, ambush! If it is poisoning, poison! You help your brothers. You help Islam any way you

like, anywhere you like! They are all kuffar, and can all be killed! Killing a kuffar who is fighting you is okay! Killing a kuffar for any reason, you can say it is okay! Even if there is no reason for it!'

And not just Abu Hamza's infamous sermon, spoken to his audience of jobless, visaless, passportless young men who were fed at the Finsbury Park mosque, who slept at the mosque, who fled the scorched dirt of Iraq, Afghanistan, Pakistan to discover that Britain wasn't a bucolic pasture of full employment, but a cold concrete maze of CCTV cameras where, with a glance, the stranger in the street convicts you. No, the triggers were everywhere. The morning of the East End riot, the BBC broadcast the notorious surveillance footage that, like four white cops bashing Rodney King outside an LA truckstop, or OJ fleeing from the choppers in his Ford Bronco, or two thirteen-year-olds at a Liverpool supermarket coaxing the toddler Jamie Bulger to his death, came to encapsulate a famously reprehensible crime. The video showed a young white man, his face obscured beneath a woollen cap, fleeing through Mornington Crescent, Camden Town, while a block away the fifteen-year-old Pakistani boy bled to death beneath a bus shelter. This image was reproduced on the *Sun's* front page, next to Malik Massawi's most recent school portrait and a photograph of the riot in full bloody bloom. In huge red letters, the headline:

CAMDEN HATE MURDER TRIGGERS
RACE RIOT

In the surveillance footage, a woollen cap concealed the

murderer's face. Four million CCTV cameras in Britain, four hundred thousand in London. Thirty-three glass eyes surveyed that four-hundred-metre stretch of pavement, but Max Lamm pulled down his hat! No forensics expert at New Scotland Yard, no digital-imaging supercomputer, can reconstruct a face the cameras never glimpsed. Now the hat was underwater in Camden Lock, its cotton lining stuffed with rocks. Or had a police diver recovered it?

Had Scotland Yard identified the murder weapon? The empty Heineken bottle that cracked a Pakistani teenager's skull.

Since his metamorphosis into Britain's most wanted new criminal, into the imagined Aryan supremacist bogeyman who, the *Daily Mail* reported, had already scared a third of the usual commuters off riding the N5 bus to Camden after dark, Max Lamm hadn't slept an hour since awakening from the nightmare of reliving his life's worst fifteen seconds. A nightmare – not merely a bad dream – because it was true. The insomnia a merciless affliction, strange after ten years of early bedtimes and 7 a.m. tennis drills, ten years of slumber assured by physical exhaustion. That physical peace was a lifetime away, as sleeplessness curdled into the pink whites of Lamm's eyes and the quartz glaze upon his cheeks. The shock all too apparent, this mistake undoing a young man who had never been violent, who hated killing and didn't eat meat for that reason, who had always brushed disorientated cicadas off the floodlit tennis court rather than squash the defenceless insects beneath his sneakers.

And this new catastrophe – the latest proof of Lamm's irrepressible predilection for disaster – had hardly begun! As he recovered from his worst year, a year of unhindered disappointment, disgrace, near-death, madness, breakdown

. . . *again* the worst had happened! And a worst far worse than any worst yet! Astonishing. That so unreasonably soon after New York, after his disintegration there, after all that had happened and just as cruelly all that hadn't, Max Lamm was descending further into the unforeseen, into the abyss he once believed would hit a rocky floor but was proving to be bottomless.

That terrifying first hour of his terrifying new life – never had an hour seemed to him so slow, so sickeningly *real* – Lamm collapsed on the N5 night bus. Boarding in Camden near the murder scene, he flashed an expired ticket, huddled up back against the heating vents, and half-drunk, he tried to think things through . . . *the kid was holding a knife . . . wasn't he? . . . he tried to steal my wallet . . . didn't he?* Already Lamm's tepid breathing, his tightened gut, the way he couldn't dismiss the catastrophe outright, told him that yes, the worst had happened. *Let me change the past!* That most mundane of prayers, desired by Max Lamm as much as anyone in the world. In the furnace of the Australian summer, he used to compulsively look for dying insects – moths, bees, scarabs, ground beetles – when he walked past dry lawns. Sometimes he spat a goblet of saliva onto a beetle stranded on its back, six legs stiff in the stifling air. Refreshed, the insect would scramble to safety. On the N5 bus, Lamm remembered a beetle resurrected by his moist embrace, yet he knew that the boy was dead. It was the way his head struck the gutter; motionless within moments, every autonomic reflex, every instinct of self-preservation, swiftly dissolved by the unintentionally fantastic accuracy of your beer bottle smashing the teenager's right temple.

Because freakishly, unintentionally, Lamm's empty Heineken bottle struck a weak spot in Malik Massawi's skull, where the temporal fossa borders the zygomatic arch of the cheekbone. As the culprit ran away, telling himself that the teenage mugger was only concussed and half-believing it too, inside the boy's skull bone fragments had in fact lesioned a cerebral artery and induced a massive subarachnoid haemorrhage. As a light rain blanketed Mornington Crescent, Malik Massawi died beneath the bus shelter.

THREE

Saturday 9 April

'*Forget if the faucets are gold and fuck me.*'

Her orders in the master bedroom. Don't ask me about the bathroom fittings. Let's do what we're here to do. What I *want you* to do. So Max Lamm did, in the finest apartment he had ever visited. Fake-tanned and contorted against the bedpost, wearing a black Gucci bra and knee socks, she was Kelly Marie Wesson. If Picasso lived in the age of the Playboy channel, his prostitutes of Montmartre would have resembled her, painted as surgically enhanced marionettes instead of real women. She posed in the way that has for millennia lured men against their better judgement, ever since antiquity's first hooker lay in reeds beside the Euphrates in 5000 BC.

But Kelly Wesson wasn't a prostitute and her favourite new boy hadn't paid a cent. To begin, we'll cut to the bones of this daughter of one of the most powerful senators in Washington. Notably statuesque among Georgetown's A-list, renowned for her wickedly suggestive smile and a sculpted peroxide bob that reminded her older admirers of Marilyn in *Gentlemen Prefer Blondes* or Jackie Kennedy circa Camelot, she was unmistakably the product of a regal American upbringing.

Kelly lived on Washington's Massachusetts Avenue, a grand leafy promenade where America's robber-barons – the Carnegies, the Morgans, the Mellons – built their faux-Roman palaces a century ago. Overlooking the stately beeches of Rock Creek Park, a pillared Victorian mansion was the cell for her solitary confinement. Kelly's only guest, once a fortnight, was L'Wren Jacques (real name: Lauren Johnson), an ex-*Vogue* stylist stuffed like a Christmas turkey with botox and collagen, who visited as a 'fashion doctor' for ninety bucks an hour. L'Wren secured next season's Prada trenchcoat, got the Lagerfeld leggings soon to hit the Parisian catwalks, or snaffled the sold-out Manolo stilettos that the other blonde socialites couldn't find, so Kelly invariably looked gorgeous in the paparazzi shots. Her sole constant accessory was enormous Dior sunglasses, inspired by Audrey Hepburn as Holly Golightly. Essential on cloudy and clear days alike, these sunglasses hid Kelly's eyes. Her pink, sick, bloodshot eyes, searching to satisfy the addictions.

Of course the money was her problem. Kelly Wesson was a petroleum heiress, not yet famous but known to upscale gossip columnists from Manhattan to the Beltway. Notorious as a seductress, she was renowned for the throaty laugh that aroused her father's friends, her male friends, even her stepbrother Dennis when he wasn't too drunk to get a boner. That *femme fatale* giggle, provocatively reminiscent of Lauren Bacall teasing Bogey in a smoky bar – and her firm bronzed breasts the shape of upturned cupcakes – did it to nearly every straight man that Kelly met, hardening them upon her command the way Pavlov's dogs salivated at the dinner bell.

And the London penthouse where she entertained

the fugitive Max Lamm? On Park Lane, overlooking the junction of Hyde Park at Marble Arch, its contents befitted the address. Teak floors swathed in handwoven rugs from a seventeenth-century Umbrian farmhouse, the stereo a futurist sculpture by Bang & Olufsen, the bathrooms awash in potpourri costing £8 a jar at Selfridges. A David Hockney landscape above the fireplace, in the study a Tiffany reading lamp (circa 1916), in the lounge room a baby Steinway (a hired pianist played it for dinner guests). Up on the roof, the hedge garden. It all belonged to Kelly's father, Senator Richard Davis Wesson. A Republican power-broker in the 2004 senate, former board member of an oil multinational and current chairman of the Senate Armed Services Committee.

Kelly's new boy admired the Jacuzzi of black marble, but she declined to run the tub. That was too risky, in case her stepsister Jacqueline returned home as they enjoyed the bubbles. Then where would he hide? The walk-in wardrobe? But, naked and wet, cupping his sodden prick, he'd drip a tell-tale trail on the carpet, just as heroic Ariadne unspooled his thread to navigate the Minotaur's labyrinth on Crete. So it was safer not to fuck in the tub.

But in this penthouse ideally suited to their luxurious tryst, when she pulled him in that warm Saturday afternoon in April 2005, he couldn't enjoy it. Not after he identified the inhibitory absence. Where was Kelly's giggle? The throaty seductive giggle she was coveted for, that from Washington to West London drove men nuts, that drove him nuts, that proclaimed '*every day handsome, wealthy, clean bachelors try to pick me up. The most eligible bachelors in London try to pick me up. But mysteriously, I've chosen you*'. Suddenly Kelly's playfulness had disappeared; no striptease, no shots of blueberry vodka, no sniffs of amyl nitrate, no cocaine snorted off the Phillipe Starck coffee table, no massages slowly descending their bodies, no tequila with lemon that she devilishly squirted upon his cock, no blowjobs, no languidly eating her pussy, no fooling about in the ways she normally initiated and they mutually enjoyed. The bedroom an army barracks, Kelly spat his orders in a sterile whisper.

'She'll be home soon. *Do it.*'

So Kelly Wesson's latest, poorest catch obsequiously slid off his jeans – black Levi's marinated in charcoal dust, sausage fat, stale canola oil – and followed her commands. He was Max Lamm; disgraced wunderkind, forgotten sporting prodigy, exiled laughing-stock, frustrated painter, currently pursued with the a £10,000-reward posted for his arrest. A libidinous failure long ago hailed, in the September 1996 edition of the *Australian Jewish News*, as the Jewish world's greatest hope for the pro tennis circuit since Aaron Krickstein, the Michigan rabbi's grandson who made the top ten in 1990. But Max Lamm no longer resembled a tennis champ; he hadn't since the frigid night in Manhattan, two Novembers earlier, when he was wheeled into the ICU at Beth Israel North, unconscious and hypothermic, after resolutely marching off a wharf at Battery Park.

Formerly muscular, once unmistakably an athlete, for two years he'd been a gaunt rake. The sole upshot of this metamorphosis being that new acquaintances, even those with a keen memory for public disgrace, seldom matched his lean, desolate face to the cherubic tennis ace who once answered to the name Max Lamm. His dark wiry hair, patchy stubble and broad plateau of a nose were unremarkable for a twenty-eight-year-old Jewish male. The yellow paint beneath Lamm's fingernails – still there though he hadn't touched a canvas in three months – were the gravestones of a talent that never bore fruit. The sensitive reddened skin encircling his nostrils – scarlet owing to a flare-up of rosacea, although for three months he'd been cold turkey – was conspicuous to nobody but a dermatologist or an observant fellow drunk. Just as subtly revealing was the slight downward elongation at the left corner of Lamm's mouth; the classic neurological indication of a bout with Bell's Palsy. The palsy – induced in London by a mystery virus *and* the drinking, back when he could at least half-finish a painting – that might return any moment.

'You're lucky,' declared the neurologist at University College hospital three weeks after Lamm walked into the A & E, tipsy at 1 p.m., with half his face numb. 'The paralysis is almost gone. In about a third of cases, it never wears off. To your dying day, you're tipping your cup sideways so the coffee doesn't run out your mouth.'

What *was* obviously unusual in Lamm's face? The eyes. His mournful hazel eyes, bleary with insomnia and perilously indiscrete. He, unlike Kelly, hadn't a fake tan, or whitened teeth from Washington's priciest orthodontist, or a covergirl hairstyle to divert a stranger's attention from *that* look. The tortured, condemned look that Lamm couldn't hide. Eyes watery, jittery, bloodshot, the pupils fogged with guilt. *It was me*, his look confessed to anybody, anything. The giveaway glance at every passerby, at every hallucinatory policeman, at every ghost, at his reflection in a cracked mirror in a public toilet in Hyde Park. He stared at that mirror for twenty-three minutes the night it happened, incredulous that suddenly his face belonged to Britain's newest, most despised murderer. A murderer who

21

hated killing, who hadn't eaten meat since the afternoon six years ago when he visited his cousin's farm in rural Victoria and spent hours talking to the gentle cows. A real nightmare had *really* occurred, and Lamm's bloodshot pupils wouldn't stop saying so.

I did it. Something irreversible, horrific. Otherworldly yet sickeningly real. Stopping me from sleeping.

Brutal.

Unforeseen.

It's making me look like *this*.

That confession alive not just in Lamm's eyes, but in the puffy bags beneath them, in his constant checking over his shoulder, in the efflux of colour from what stubbornly remained — no matter the stubble, the barbeque grease, the scarred red nose, the numb right corner of his lips — the face of a decent-looking kid from Caulfield, the leafy Melbourne suburb where in many streets, every house has a *mezuzah* nailed to its front doorpost. The *mezuzah* — a tiny scroll of Torah scripture wrapped inside a cigar-sized cylinder — that proclaims to the passerby: *this is not merely a house. It is a home. A Jewish home. So watch what you do and say.*

Lamm's fucking eyes. They hadn't shut up in three nights since the alleged murder, and they said it was too late to fix anything. Much too late.

FOUR

Thursday 7 April

Tottenham Court Road, the morning *it* happened. Start at the grimy gridlocked junction at Oxford Street, arguably the sickest of central London's arteries. Dirt, dust, refuse, rubbish flood the street like the grey clouds rain polystyrene. A wraparound billboard, the breadth of a 737's wingspan, showcases a pale prepubescent model pouting in her Calvin Klein underwear. Opposite, the cavernous *G-A-Y* club at the Astoria where, a cold April night five years earlier, the deranged neo-Nazi David Copeland stalked his quarry until he planted a nail bomb in a nearby gay pub, the Admiral Duncan, killing two men and a pregnant woman.

By the early years of the new millennium, London had arisen from the operating table and its cosmetic surgery was botched. Like other financial centres, the capital got a tummy tuck, a facelift and a colostomy bag, separating the healthy flesh from the shit. A few blocks north of the crime scene, Chalk Farm's decrepit council estates shelter hooded teenagers who aspire to the cheap martyrdom of hip-hop assassination. Ten minutes' walk south reveals Primrose Hill's velvety boutiques, cute coffee bars and terraces with a lap pool. This whitewashed island of affluence assured by good schools, trust funds and the institutionalized apprehension of disorder.

Now ride the N5 bus back west. Wednesday through Saturday nights, Soho's Old Compton Street is jammed by tourists on pub crawls, gay men revelling in their unashamed abundance, lycra-clad backpackers hawking rides on fibre-glass rickshaws, shivering transsexual hookers sucking cigarettes in stilettos; all crowding the pavements, cafés, bars, dance floors until 4 or 5 a.m. when finally the cost of one more vodka, the purifying limits of the human kidney, and the pervasive stench of all that piss – nine parts ethanol to one part water, pooled in doorways stinking like an unwashed kennel – sends everyone home to bed or to sleep in the gutter.

It was 4.34 a.m. by Lamm's wristwatch when a horde of drunk backpackers – Spaniards, Italians, Israelis, Australians, Canadians, New Zealanders yelling uproariously after a typical Soho beer binge – boarded the bus for their short ride to Bayswater. Back to their budget hostels or decrepit digs in crumbling Edwardian mansions rented, room by room, to frugal travellers or to pimps and their duped doped girls smuggled in from Albania. Amongst the hirsute twentysomethings yabbering in six languages, Lamm couldn't concentrate. He couldn't deconstruct, reconstruct, couldn't re-live the worst fifteen seconds of his life, couldn't recall the moment when the boy collapsed, couldn't work out what had *really* just happened, or strategize a way out through the tightening net – *couldn't think* – when three feet away in the intoxicated prime of their unjaded youth, the toothy backpackers laughed like hyenas, smooched each other, translated 'fuck I'm drunk' into their mother tongues, admired each other's henna tattoos, facial piercings

24

and dreadlocks, or, underneath the seats, submitted to what their beer-saturated guts naturally had to do. It's always a party at the United Nations of vomit.

Lamm decided to sit on the upper deck. He pulled up his jacket hood and shuffled though the crowd. But the stairs were blocked by a heap of enormous backpacks belonging to five Spaniards asking the way to Heathrow. In the driver's perspex booth, Lamm noticed, was a Siemens ticket machine with a computer screen, a GPS receiver, an LCD display of traffic updates, weather reports, police alerts, ticket prices . . . a glowing array befitting the control room of a nuclear submarine. And there, flashing on the screen in bold type: METROPOLITAN POLICE ALERT.

Straining his neck, Lamm overheard the driver's short-wave radio. *Police are investigating a fatal attack on Mornington Cre . . .* – a passenger's Spanish yelp eclipsed the next few words – *a search is underway. The suspect is described as light-skinned, approximately six feet tall, wearing black jeans, a dark red jacket . . .*

The boy's dead.

The surveillance cameras saw you.

Two blocks down Bayswater Road, blue lights flashed. A police van.

The driver's already made the call? You're *that* conspicuous?

At Lancaster Gate the doors opened. Yielding to the same instinct for self-preservation that propelled the bottle into the teenage mugger's skull, Lamm joined the back-packers disembarking. Twenty sozzled Swedes staggered to their hostels as he scampered over the fence into Hyde Park. Hunted, haunted Lamm! Run through the flowerbed, behind a knobbled birch. Headlights approaching; *stay still!*

Crouching in bushes, Lamm allowed himself a piss that, during the past hour's giddy recollection of not much at all, somehow hadn't innervated the nerve pathways from his swollen bladder up to his brain. His bewilderment so total, he hadn't felt the need to urinate. Hadn't *felt* that he felt the need to urinate.

Soaking the scrub and probably his sneakers, Lamm saw the police lights on Bayswater Road. Lights that – owing to a suspicious vehicle, a terrorist alert or a constable's pizza getting cold – might any moment spin 360 degrees, flashing, sirens hollering, thereby reassuring the residents of West London's best streets (the PM's newly purchased mansion only a few blocks away in Connaught Square) that they could sleep soundly, if they could get back to sleep. Degenerate, disorientated Lamm! He stared at the blue and white glare atop the police car's roof, and only then – hollowed by hunger and exhaustion into an unresponsive vessel, seeing blurry lilac dots flashing at the back of his eyelids – did he realize that this piss-soaked shrub, and the knee-high lavender bushes surrounding it, was, in fact, a very foolish place to hide.

Into bushes sticky, black as tar, running, ducking, until he collapsed beneath a weeping willow. *Keep going?* He got up, paced circles, trying to believe what he knew had happened, was happening, could happen, then sat again, stood again, collapsed, got up, debating where to flee and how and when. The why was unquestionable. Drenched in sweat amid the cold fogging his breath, Lamm staggered into the frigid starlit undergrowth, hearing the whirring rat-a-tat of a helicopter – a police helicopter – not far off, getting louder, that might sweep its floodlight through Hyde Park. *They knew he was here?* How? Could the bus driver really have identified the murder suspect among the throng of passengers?

Another ten minutes Lamm stumbled left, right, left, left . . . fleeing the German shepherds that might enter the park, might catch his scent . . . run deeper into this labyrinthine dark of necessity! Into this darkness timelessly dark, so unsettlingly natural in the midst of London's neon plastic playground. Yet after nightfall who gives a shit? *Who's here?* Only squirrels, foxes, birds at roost, the homeless schizophrenics asleep beneath a tree in summer and occasionally frozen dead in winter, and perhaps a few Tory MPs fucking anonymous men in the shrubbery.

At the park's eastern corner, the helicopter hovered down. Two silvery searchlights rupturing its belly, rotors blurring the starless sky. *They've seen you?* Into the brush, thorns ripping Lamm's forearms. Blood. *Faster!* Another path (or the overgrown semblance of a path) marked by a brambleless cleavage through the bushes. Running, swerving as the deathly glare chopped closer. What did your bastard of a tennis coach always say? *Choose the path of least resistance.*

Finally a clump of undergrowth thick enough for a hiding place. Like a fox eluding bloodthirsty toffs, into the bush Lamm crawled, refreshed by the fertile embrace of dew upon his cheeks. Who ventures here but the rats? *Now wait.* For a deafening few seconds, the silhouettes of leaves projected onto the muddy backs of his hands while the blinding searchlight hovered above.

Darkness. The pitch of the thundering rat-a-tat dropped precipitously as the helicopter veered north.

Lying in the wet dirt, absurdly Lamm recalled the scientific explanation: as the helicopter hovers away, its noise decreases in pitch because the soundwaves stretch as they travel farther to your ears. That's why the chopper made a lower-pitched sound as it flew off. Simple. Elegant. Eternal.

'*It's called the Doppler effect.*'

Correct. Lamm heard those words spoken aloud, and he jolted. The park's most terrifying sound yet. Terrifying not for a reason concerning elementary physics, nor the manhunt for a murderer, but because that simple explanatory sentence – '*It's called the Doppler effect*' – was spoken, unmistakably, by a man who had died ten years ago.

FIVE

The suicidal absurdity of regarding anything but this moment! Of considering anything but the danger! Yet the words in Lamm's ears – '*It's called the Doppler effect*' – were too recognizable; that blunt voice belonged to his favourite high school teacher, Mr Lewski.

Mr Lewski, who never woke up the last day of semester in November 1995.

Your dead tenth-grade teacher returns to life, the night that yours disintegrates! At 5.03 a.m. in a wet bush while you're hunted like a fox. Hyde Park is Mr Lewski's posthumous classroom. His students the squirrels, his blackboard a blackberry bush.

There!

Beneath the gargantuan weeping willow, pixelated by the moonlight's sheen – or Lamm's hallucinatory optic nerve? – was Lewski. Lewski's ghost. Or in your mind's eye, the mirage of a ghost? Whatever it was, it *was* Mr Lewski: the deceased intellectual battering ram of a tenth-grade teacher. There, standing in the impoverished grass shaded by the willow's mournful dreadlocks, was Mr Lewski who had been gone ten years!

The teacher's ghost shimmered in his prickly white beard, horn-rimmed glasses, scuffed loafers and the too-big herringbone suit he wore stiff on the dais at speech nights and stiff inside a wooden box in November 1995, dead at sixty-three from a carcinoma the same week that Yitzhak Rabin was assassinated (until Rabbi Gringlass interceded at the funeral home to ensure that Lewski was instead buried in *tachrichim*, the Jewish burial shrouds of white linen and nothing else). Mr Lewski with the bombshell daughter Romy, the one-in-a-hundred natural blonde faux-*shiksa*, whose beach-bunny looks – for a Jewish girl the genetic lightning strike of golden hair and Russ Meyer tits that, people said, could only be the result of a mix-up in the maternity ward – fuelled fantasies for most of the boys (and a few girls) at Mount Scopus College. Frustratingly, Romy Lewski was the teacher's daughter and hence as off-limits as Svetlana Stalin was to her own father's underlings, unless the horny *apparachniks* wanted twenty years breaking boulders out on the womanless Siberian wastes.

Silent, stupefied Lamm! Do you wait for your teacher's spectre to say something? *Or say it yourself?* Was Lamm's terror – this phantom's horrific realness imperceptible from reality – what the schizophrenic homeless bum endures daily? In New York, Lamm often observed a few vagrants near the shelter at St Mark's Place, enthroned on park benches amid their kingdom of pigeons and ghosts. Each man a stinking tortured anonymity, mumbling to himself beneath an avalanching beard and dreadlock crown.

Yet, whether truly a supernatural visitation in Hyde Park or the hallucinatory depths to Lamm's encroaching madness, it *was* Mr Lewski! The quietly heroic teacher who lectured enthrallingly even ten minutes before the final bell on a Friday afternoon, who led classroom discussion of the high school English standards – *Of Mice and Men, Gatsby,*

The Outsiders, The Crucible – in allegiance to his unshakable assumption that: (a) his students were booklovers, critics, *thinkers* whether they knew it or not; (b) a love of language lurked untapped within every kid even if they hated to read; and (c) his students were innately receptive to a stimulating classroom debate, and weren't itching for the bell so they could rush to McDonald's or the shopping mall or the TV set.

Uncompromising at comprehension, unforgettable for never forgetting *anything*, peerless in the way he pushed his favourite texts – in science labs the passages from Newton's *Opticks* or Darwin's journals as examples of inferential genius, or in English class the excerpts from Steinbeck, Isaac Beshavis Singer, Auden, Patrick White – the way a mother stuffs her toddler with mashed banana. *That* was Mr Lewski. Who, after thirty-three years of teaching *Of Mice and Men*, knew George and Lennie's two-handers by heart, yet with inexhaustible enthusiasm punctured any fifteen-year-old's apathy to that masterful novella about two itinerant farmhands doomed not by the Depression's dustbowl, but their defiance of it.

Before the night Mr Leswki appeared – materialized? – in Hyde Park, Lamm last saw him during the final school week of 1995. Nauseous from chemotherapy, a frayed bush hat shielding his hairless head from the merciless Australian sun, too weak to walk without his daughters propping his arms, Lewski took a final stroll through the schoolyard. Waving hello, shaking hands, smiling like he'd won a marathon, quizzing a few kids about the books he'd taught; nothing to alarm the students who, if they knew the facts, would get teary on the spot. He noticed Lamm out on the football oval. 'Hiya Max!' Lewski yelled hoarsely. *It's*

okay. We'll talk another time. Don't bother yourself to come over.
So Lamm didn't; he waved hello and kept up the sweaty
wordless rhythm of kick-to-kick.

At assembly that Thursday, Principal Rubin announced
that Mr Lewski had passed away. There would be a *minyan*
in the school synagogue at seven o'clock. Lewski's final
act as a teacher was banning mobile phones from his classroom. In 1995 the mobile phone – back then a big plastic
brick – was slowly commencing its nefarious ransacking of
the literary tradition. Presciently, Mr Lewski recognized the
threat of the Motorola's abbreviated text-talk, as destructive
to the language he loved – the language of Shakespeare and
Milton, Auden and Hemingway – as the damned metastatic
carcinoma was to his own body, eating him inside out.

Mr Lewski discovered his illness too late, but he was
early to predict the mobile phone's gangrenous infection of
comprehension, of the English language, that disintegrates
living words into dry, monosyllabic bones. 'This ultra-
abbreviated form of communication,' Mr Lewski announced
to his students, 'will cause the decay of written discourse,
of concise expression, of critical *thinking*.' A decade later,
sixteen-year-olds from Delhi to Delaware unashamedly
write 'you' as 'U', 'for' as '4', substitute '2' for 'to', click
a smiley-faced icon for a description of joy or a sad-faced
icon for a pang of disappointment, haven't read a document
more profound than their mobile payment plan and
generally achieve literary comprehension similar to that
acquired by chimpanzees in psychology labs who learn sign
language from infancy.

Mr Lewski made the pre-emptive strike. In his classroom,
years before any other classroom at Mount Scopus College
or indeed any classroom in Melbourne, mobile phones were

banned. Gallantly he assaulted the hypnotic hegemony of Gameboys, GameGears, Walkmen and Nokias. He won his battle.

'John Steinbeck is forthright about Lennie's disability' Mr Lewski proclaimed in class one Wednesday morning in 1994, and again as a ghost in Hyde Park on the opening night of Lamm's worst catastrophe.

'Lennie Small is Steinbeck's portrayal of the type of person that we used to call *simple*. Now they're not simple, they're complicated and you call them intellectually disabled. But to Steinbeck, Lennie's simple. He's a six-year-old in a giant's body. Okay, we know what was wrong with Lennie. But what was *right* with him?'

'He didn't mean to kill Curley's wife.'

Gasps. Eyebrows shot upwards. The students shocked. Because this was a voice seldom heard in English class: Martin Weinberg, the bad egg of Mount Scopus. A wiry-haired hulk of sixteen who, if he wasn't suspended for smoking pot in the lane behind the gym, or starting fights in the schoolyard, or skipping school at the racetrack with his disreputable *schnorer* of a father Lou (a tax lawyer who, the other parents agreed, worked for criminals and would end up in an acid bath or wearing concrete boots at the bottom of Port Phillip Bay) was usually vandalizing school desks with a drawing compass and chewing beef jerky; the beef jerky being a *treif* no-no that drove Gringlass the school rabbi nuts.

Martin Weinberg – destined to ignominiously perpetuate the Jewish gangster lineage of Meyer Lansky, Bugsy Siegel, Longy Zwillman, et al – frequently sat next to Lamm in English class. Weinberg the notorious troublemaker who broke the PE teacher's nose with a cricket ball, then claimed it was an accident. Weinberg who, a week earlier, scandalously chose for his poetry recital *that* notorious poem by Philip Larkin while the other students memorized safe choices like Shakespeare's 'Shall I compare thee to a summer's day' sonnet, or Auden's *Funeral Blues* that they'd heard in the funeral scene of a romantic comedy, or a rabbi-approved lamentation from King Solomon's *Ecclesiastes*, or a confusing classic recommended by their parents – Keats, Yeats, the Beats – certain to earn polite applause and at least a B+. Not Martin Weinberg, who typed 'fuck poetry' into a primitive search engine and, pleased that a result appeared, was immediately entranced by the blunt intuitive force of Larkin's verse.

Who better to have written those three searing stanzas, so bludgeoningly precise in their misanthropy, misogyny, misery – the whole life-affirming shebang of that critically endangered species, the Chauvinist of Letters – but a lifelong provincial librarian like Philip Larkin? For thirty years a writer surrounded by the men he cherished – Hardy, Eliot, Lawrence – rotting unborrowed on the shelves, while parents requested the same sickly-sweet sedatives for their children (Enid Blyton and *The Babysitters Club* most often on loan). Larkin hunched at the library desk in his tweed jacket and corduroy slacks, observing eighteen-year-old girls (not yet women), fresh from the university dormitories, reading *The Times* for free and giggling at Harold Wilson's bad teeth. Girls cloaking their spindly white legs, their pale fulsome breasts that Larkin so loved, in dowdy long skirts and shapeless brown cardigans that maintained the impotent dreariness of the University of Hull while, at bigger colleges elsewhere in Britain, sexual intercourse began in 1963.

In English class, Martin Weinberg recited Philip Larkin's

poem that, were his teacher anyone at Mount Scopus College but Mr Lewski, would have got him suspended for the third time that semester:

They fuck you up, your mum and dad . . .

Speechless, the students stared at each other. *Hear that? Weinberg said fuck!* Fuck, the reigning king of four-letter words (shit being the populist princess kissing toddlers in the streets; cunt the queen mother who won't leave her palatial bedroom). Fuck. A word forbidden, of course, by Principal Rubin. Swear in the classroom, you clean the schoolyard after school. Nevertheless, Mr Lewski – an island of passion for making the students *think for themselves* – did the unthinkable.

'Martin, a very interesting choice. Let's hear it again.'

Recite the whole dirty poem *again*! Larkin's naughty rhymes and all, and fuck Principal Rubin's after-school detention for saying a word for the copulatory act that had, after all, long been embraced by the lewd literary lineage from Joyce, Henry Miller, Hemingway up to fucking P Roth and fugging N Mailer. Obediently, Martin Weinberg re-read Larkin's paean to parentlessness. His twenty-nine classmates listened intently, nodding, for these sixteen-year-olds were, after all, in the midst of their own hormonal upheavals against parental hypocrisy and pimpleless skin. *They fuck you up, your mum and dad.* Do they ever.

Two months later, Mr Lewski opens his dog-eared *Of Mice and Men*. Fire burning in the centre of his circular spectacles.

'What I want to know is, what was *right* with Lennie?'

'He didn't mean to kill Curley's wife.'

Martin Weinberg answers a question in English class! *That* was Mr Lewski. The other students couldn't have been more surprised had Weinberg produced a prayer book from his jeans, along with the cigarettes, flick-knife and knuckledusters, then faced Jerusalem and *davvened* fluently as the Yeshivah boys in their black suits. Astonishing that under Mr Lewski's guidance, Mount Scopus College's worst-behaved kid had an opinion about literature. Not the odds at the dog track, nor the way to beat somebody with a rubber hose, but literature! And not the type you get wrapped in black plastic off the newsagent's top shelf.

'Lennie wanted to fit in at the ranch,' Weinberg mumbled, stabbing his desk with a dry ballpoint. 'He couldn't change himself. Lennie was dumb but innocent.'

The other kids will know you've read the book. Fuck them.

'Lennie didn't *mean* to kill Curly's wife. But the other men didn't care. They didn't care that Lennie was, like, a big ignorant kid. If George hadn't done it, they would've shot Lennie themselves.'

The school's bad egg analyses a novel as near perfect as a novel gets; even the heroic teacher is surprised. The reach of the well-written word reminds Lewski: *this is why you're here.* To these sixteen-year-olds, Mr Lewski is the last upright pillar in civilization's crumbling Acropolis of paper and ink, of meanings, of ideas beyond the brown-as-shit obvious. The last pillar standing in the grand decaying temple of words, of what words do, of imaginative genius spanning the Greek tragedies, the Mahabharata, the Talmud up to the volumes of Dickens in the bargain bin at your local bookstore. The invaluable temple of literature, buckling beneath all the Gameboys and mobile phones and pocket TVs amassing on its roof like a billion plastic diamonds raining from heaven.

'Thank you, Martin, yours is a voice that we want to hear

more of. Now, who can suggest why Steinbeck's drifters play dumb when they arrive at the ranch? What mistake has Lennie *already* made at the book's beginning?'

Another student answered, but Mr Lewski stared at Weinberg, back at carving his desk with a drawing cornpass. Who'd have thought the kid gave a shit? And watching Mr Lewski watching Weinberg, Max Lamm recognized the unadulterated joy he'd observed in toddlers running head-first into a sprinkler on a hot summer's day, a good ten years before they grew up enough to stop being happy. Mr Lewski stood there staring at the most insolent, disagreeable kid he'd ever taught, enraptured the way the black-hatters at the Yeshiva, the bearded Orthodox with their nine kids in a Toyota van, would feel if they chanced upon the Messiah late one Friday afternoon at the deli while they waited for pickled herring.

How, Max Lamm wondered that moment in the classroom and again eleven years later with the teacher's ghost in Hyde Park, did Mr Lewski sustain his unforced love of learning? For thirty-four years, the enlightenment he experienced through enlightening others. The unartificial effervescence that Lewski applied not only to educating his students, but to life as a whole! A man whose existence, it was obvious now that Lamm's had disintegrated, had been phenomenally charged with charity, selflessness, responsibility, common sense. *The right priorities.*

That's what invigorated your English teacher; an ordered life. Cohesion from chaos; the noble challenge of moulding critical young minds against the relentless flood of informationless info, of manufactured news, of encrypted advertising that submerges the kids every time they turn on the TV. Never won a bravery award like the guy who saved your life in the East River, but Lewski *was* a hero. He battled stupidity's entropy, the ignorance implicit in assumptions. *Order against disorder.* That was your teacher's oxygen until the cancer won. Mr Lewski was everything that you're not.

In the wet bushes, the teacher's ghost – or your hallucination? – shimmered in the lilac hue of the chopper's distant searchlight.

'*Mr Lewski!*'

Lamm shouted the teacher's name, aware that he was, of course, giving away his hiding place. This is the way they'll catch you? He remembered a story he read in *New Scientist* magazine at a chiropractor's waiting room. A team of physicists, from Lawrence Livermore or another of the Pentagon's military weapons labs, had researched how to use lasers to make sounds in the sky. Their aim was to simulate Allah's voice in the clouds above Saddam's armies, thunderously instructing the soldiers to leave Kuwait and go home for prayers.

'*Mr Lewski!*'

No reply.

Gone. But the tweed jacketed phantom remained burnt into Lamm's retinas.

It *was* a ghost? Because if merely a figment of psychosis, then Mr Lewski would've said something? Crazy people hear voices, right?

Lewski stared at you silently. The ghost of condemnation.

SIX

Throughout Hyde Park, the police helicopter whirred like a mosquito through a radio. After twenty minutes of creeping through dewy foliage, Lamm trampled into an overgrown grove. The width of half a tennis court, its uncut grass bathed a sepia hue beneath pregnant purple clouds and smog eclipsing stars. At the centre a barbeque; this was once a pleasant, lavender-scented grotto ideal for picnics in springtime. Not so popular now that four fried chicken franchises crowded the block between Selfridges and Great Cumberland Place. The barbeque's knobs, Lamm noticed, were crisscrossed with stale spider webs.

Streaks of dawn pierced the fog. He sat atop the filthy forgotten grille. Rubbed his numb feet, exhaled, and thought: this new life. This abhorrent new life because the poor fucker's dead. What might have saved the kid? Neurosurgery? *You killed him.* Say a prayer, murmur *kaddish* at the dribbling sky. Do you remember the words?

Comatose pupils don't dilate like *that*, like a leaky hose. Time decays in one direction. Lamm recalled the dull lifeless thud of Malik Massawi's head striking the gutter. The stillness, the disconcerting lack of bleeding. The glassy absence in those brown eyes fixed at the bus shelter's perspex roof. It didn't take a physician to discern that the essence of survival – the dull clack-clack-clack of being alive, like a train on worn tracks – had irretrievably disappeared when the Pakistani boy lay on the Camden pavement like an undersized fish asphyxiated on the floor of a sinking dingy.

The helicopter had returned. In less than a minute loudening from a distant buzz to thunder overhead, its searchlights crisscrossing the park. Discernible in the spotlight's spill: METROPOLITAN POLICE in blue letters beneath the cockpit. Lamm crouched behind the barbeque. *Run into the bushes? Or stay still?* The rat-a-tat loudened, leaves shuddering in the gale of rotors two hundred metres away. *Crawl for cover? But they'll see you!*

Lamm noticed an iron grate set into the barbeque's limestone base. He pulled at the rusty hinge, tripping backwards when the latch gave way. Inside, a shallow cavity containing gas pipes. Not fit for a temporary grave, but inside it he crawled. In apartments overlooking Hyde Park, bedside lamps flickered on as hedge fund managers and PR executives awoke to the chopper's racket. This fucking noise at four-thirty in the morning! There's a doorman downstairs, surveillance cameras in the elevators, still a searchlight's piercing my curtains!

The light hit the old barbeque. Nothing.

Nine hours Lamm stayed down there. Sleeping thirty, forty minutes at a time, his eyes fleshy pink bulbs, the hunger and headache unprecedented. This hunger making Lamm giddy, its hollow intestinal tentacles climbing up, up his throat to suck everything from anything. Too exhausted to risk buying food; he'd climbed outside once already, to piss and dump the trash left by the hole's previous degenerate tenant. Too dangerous for his flat in Golders Green, the one-bedroom rental where his rotting mattress grew an undiscovered species of mould, where fat termites devoured the chipboard mantelpiece. The hundred-quid-a-fortnight place that Lamm shared – at least for that month – with a typically hairy, stoned Israeli backpacker named Avi. What if the police had somehow identified him from the CCTV footage? What if they had collected his DNA from the crime scene and made a match to a database that he didn't know existed? They might be watching his address.

Or they haven't identified you?

Either Lamm remained anonymous, or the area was under surveillance unmatched since the Hyde Park bombing of 1982, when an IRA nail bomb killed four men and seven horses of the Queen's Household Cavalry parade.

If you fall asleep, the hypothermia's guaranteed. So, when Lamm heard only squirrels clawing oaks and the faint hum of Oxford Street taxis, he crawled outside. With his lighter (dry in a crushed pack of Marlboros), he lit the gas barbeque at 'medium' on the dial. A cruel end for the spiders roasting inside (yet no crueller than being eaten by your mother, as baby spiders often are). Twenty minutes later when he turned off the gas, the subterranean hideout was warm as a Park Lane penthouse. Down the hole, Lamm loosened his scarf and exhaled like a walrus.

Your alarm might go off! Lamm fumbled for his mobile phone, encased in dust. But it wouldn't turn on; the battery was flat. Lamm bit his tongue. *You were meant to charge it last night!* And the charger is on your bedside table, plugged into the one reliable socket in your decaying bedroom. Yes, there are phone boxes along Bayswater Road, decorated with prostitutes' flyers showcasing women photocopied from Russian porn magazines. But it's too dangerous to leave the park.

And who would you call?

His jacket hood a pillow, Lamm lay on the toasted bricks. Sleep, until your nails grow like a badger's and skin covers your eyes like a mole's! He looked up through the grill at the glowing coals. Funny, the way those hot rocks look fuzzily unreal, like an oil painting in the subterranean dim. The blurry coals of hell, as depicted in the Renaissance masterworks – Rubens, Caravaggios, Raphaels, et al – that his art teacher, Ms Komesaroff, stuck on the walls of the painting room at Mount Scopus College. Always she praised the overblown religious imagery in those sixteenth-century oils – Adam and Eve, archangels and apples, serpents and Satan – all the Pope-appeasing excess that Principal Rubin and Rabbi Gringlass appreciated as Great Art, instead of the degenerate works – the bloody aneurysmic hell of Hieronymus Bosch, the gory Goyas, or something contemporary like a bloodlusty Francis Bacon or a technicolour collage of posh Gilbert and George fucking each other in the arse – that engrossed Lamm in their glorious transgression.

Max Lamm: sports champ *and* a lover of art. A combo that typically gets annihilated in the one person the way matter and antimatter disappear in a flash of light. Ms Komesaroff pasted Caravaggio's portrayals of hell upon the art room walls, but, Rabbi Gringlass informed the students, Jews don't really believe in hell. Hell's for drunk Irish priests and nuns blessing their spaghetti in the Vatican courtyard. The Jewish hell – the most recent Jewish hell in the four-thousand-year-old lineage of Jewish hells – was sixty years ago. If Hieronymus Bosch saw Adolf Eichmann's handiwork, he couldn't paint it. No paint's bloody enough for the blood, black enough for the black.

Order vs disorder. At Lamm's core was the instinctive force – a raw non-negotiable force – betraying the grey world of rules, regulations, polite expectations. The timeless pull of heroic failure: *that's* what intoxicates you. For thirteen years, from adolescence until he tried to drown himself in the East River, Lamm was consumed by: (1) competitiveness, incorporating his mysterious talent for tennis; (2) painting, as he tried to portray on canvas his warped love of the female form; and (3) the fleshy gash revealed by a statuesque girl's thighs akimbo, during the final prepenetrative moments before primal anticipation yields to the urge's clockwork thrust.

At Melbourne University Law School and again when he took a semester at NYU, the obese volumes of legislation numbed those human impulses. Numbed the uncooked essence of existence – *flee, fight, fuck* – portrayed in the paintings he loved. The paintings in expensive books that, when he was fifteen years old, Lamm permanently borrowed from the art room at Mount Scopus. After three hours of gazing at the monotonous baseline, service line, net, at fuzzy yellow balls bouncing blurry top spins, Lamm relaxed not as his fellow tennis champs did – i.e., watching TV sports or blabbering over a $17 salad in a chrome café – but by sitting in leafy Caulfield Park on the way home and losing himself in those canvasses; the depraved images that confused his father, to whom art meant the *Mona Lisa* and the painting of dogs playing poker.

Since his schooldays raiding the bookshelf in Ms Komesaroff's art room, Lamm had loved Francis Bacon.

Bacon's green gorilla skulls atop stark slabs of meat, his bloody purple rendering of Pope Innocent X on a melting gold throne, his mouthy pink coathangers of fleshy Soho queens decamped on garish beds of blood, cum, saliva, sweat. A lot beautifully, truthfully pornographic in Bacon's convulsions of bones, lips, cocks, skin; revoltingly animal yet arousingly human. Bacon's orgasmic deathly eruptions spoke to Lamm, to a black cranny inside this nice Jewish boy, and Lamm aped the master's technique – the burst aneurysms of white, the haemorrhaging globules of congealed red – when he spent six months working on a canvas of a terrified fox fleeing its hunting party. Lamm loved Goya too. *Los Desastres de la Guerra* illustrating what soldiers do when violence becomes victory's end, not its means. Disembowelment. Dismemberment. Decapitation. How superbly, *lovingly*, Goya etches a cockless, headless body draped over a tree stump! Or *La Maja Desnuda*, the first totally profane nude in Western art, portraying the Spanish master's plump mistress begging for it.

What most captivated Lamm in Ms Komesaroff's art room, so that he slipped *The Collected Paintings of Francisco Goya* into his schoolbag, was *Saturn Devouring his Son*. Naked wild-haired Saturn, the Roman god of agriculture (who resembles an unwashed homeless bum) is tearing his baby son into pieces. Ripping the infant's head off, arms and neck too, drenched in newborn fluids, inside a dim cavern not dissimilar to the hole beneath a barbeque in Hyde Park. Saturn devours the son who, it had been prophesised, would overthrow his father. Deaf, hallucinating with encephalitis, Goya painted the cannibalistic horror onto a wall in his villa 'Quinta del Sordo' – the 'House of the Deaf Man' – by the Manzanares River outside Madrid.

Beneath Hyde Park, Lamm saw that painting shimmer in the barbeque's orange coals. The way Goya portrays the bloodstained, shitstained wound of a wasted existence. The wound of your mistakes consuming you, so that you eat your future, your son; *that's* the fact fogged over by respectable Law. The ugliness! A savage truth concealed by the volumes of legislature, professional practice, tax guidelines and precedents that you were told to study two hours a night. Two hours' staring at the impenetrable page, at the jargon . . . *a tale told by an idiot, full of sound and fury. Signifying nothing.* Macbeth knew the same infernal frustration.

New York University, February 2003. Max Lamm with haunted pink eyes, sitting up the back of a lecture in international criminal law. He pretended to ignore the jeers, sneers, sniggers sent his way by classmates, lecturers, even Sergei the janitor who evidently read the *New York Post* sports pages. The scandal broke and inevitably, Lamm was asked to 'take time off'. The first exchange student ever expelled from New York University Law School. Sure, Ted Kennedy was expelled from Harvard and returned to graduate. But Ted Kennedy was a Kennedy. Walking out of the law school's grand lobby for the last time, Lamm glimpsed the future, how he'd likely be remembered: not as a tennis champ upon the winner's podium, nor as a crusading attorney, painter, writer, thinker, animal lover, renaissance man-child of exceptional unrequited talents, but as the downloaded ghoul who lost his student visa by fucking a Salvadorian beauty on a concave bed in an illegal whorehouse on Second Avenue.

Of Max Lamm's innate qualities – the aptitude for tennis, his ability with a paintbrush, his natural appreciation for art, his uncompromising empathy for animals, his tendency to see the heart of a matter (and to ignore it) – the most exceptional was his preponderance for catastrophe. *No one's good at everything, no one's good at nothing.* A saying of his mother's, before the lymphoma stole her, when out shopping they'd see a busker drumming an upturned garbage bin with two plastic forks, or watch a performance artist (the hairy creative type in hessian pantaloons) balancing a bowling pin on his forehead. The kind lady that she was, Ruth Lamm threw the street performers a dollar or three.

'Bravo. Don't knock your teeth out,' she'd yell at unicyclists, contortionists, acrobats doing circus tricks on Bourke Street Mall. 'Max, don't *ever* try that yourself.'

Who did she hurt? The question tiny cousin Sarah, twelve years old with a Hollywood lisp, asked Rabbi Gurwitz at the funeral. Like the rabbi was a Supreme Court judge who might reverse the untimely passing. Eleven years ago, Lamm's mother was sick for nineteen months. Beginning in the marrow, her immune system ate itself.

It took Malik Massawi a second. *Before you realized it.*

Before he realized it.

How long did your backhand volley take?

A half-second? Fifth of a second?

Your backhand volley with a beer bottle.

The horrific thing, perpetrated by someone whose predisposition for disaster is insatiable.

That fatal beer bottle. Where is it now?

Probably in a forensics lab. It could have picked up a trace of your DNA.

Forget it. You're safe here.

Sleep!

Now!

He couldn't. You try not to think of a pink elephant and one thing comes to mind.

7.24 a.m. The Pakistani boy died three hours ago.

How did the kid materialize like that? From where?

The street was empty. Then there's the dead boy when he wasn't dead. In Camden the muggers step out of thin air.

A big boy for fifteen. He'll need a big coffin.

What do Muslims call their coffins? Or do they cremate their dead?

Lamm remembered watching a BBC programme about the Zoroastrians of Iran. An ancient sect, pre-dating Islam, who expose their dead atop a sacred hill south of Tehran. The corpses uncovered between life and death, consumed by vultures.

The empty beer bottle awaited you like the sword in the stone.

The boy flicked his knife.

Your wallet. Now!

He would have stabbed you. He had a knife.

He had a knife?

He did or he didn't.

Lamm remembered reading about that black guy killed in New York a few years ago. Amadou Diallo, dead on the cover of *Time* magazine. Shot in the chest by the NYPD because his wallet looked like a gun.

You made the same mistake.

The boy had a knife!

Maybe. You should've checked. He fell down so fucking fast.

Why did your bottle do that?

Because of the thousands of glass bottles wielded by drunks around the world that morning in April 2005, Lamm's prenaturally, freakishly, hit the sweet spot. Slightly

47

above the ear, at the coronal suture of the frontal and parietal bones. Lamm watched the kid collapsing, that millisecond of astonishment when you trip, you fall over and in mid-air you realize: *I will bleed*. Lamm never aimed the bottle; it was a perfect volley skimming the baseline. The severe, unthought wrist movement that he practised daily for fourteen years; the shot would have been a winner. *Thwack*. Years ago that reflex made him a wunderkind, almost a success, and in a deserted Camden street it took him down.

Astonishing. Lamm couldn't fool himself, not in a space so oppressive – so very much like a coffin – as beneath this barbeque. He exhaled, bemoaning what was intolerable: not only that he killed a Pakistani teenager, the despair, the hunger, the darkness, the claustrophobic hideout beneath a barbeque grease trap and the best efforts of the Metropolitan Police. It was New York too. The twelve minutes of emotionless resolve, a little over two years ago, when he walked into the East River. 9th April, 2003. The night Baghdad fell, although at 3 a.m. when Lamm marched into the frigid filthy current, the Pentagon hadn't yet announced their Pyrrhic victory. The East River so cold that Lamm bit his tongue, tasting blood's iron tang amid the icy blackness. He trudged farther, deeper in, dragged by the current and not fighting it.

But in that freezing dirty water, Lamm felt the warm salty waves he rode as a boy every summer at Jan Juc beach. His translucent swell, where the temperate surf pulled him down unfailingly, reassuringly, until he got dumped on the shore, ears full of sand, fingertips pickled like baby onions, while his mother sunbaked and gazed into the shy pinprick eyes of sand crabs. No matter how far out he swam, the waves of Bass Strait brought him in; those failsafe foaming lifeguards, their salty embrace stinging Lamm's chapped lips, that eighteen years later in the East River metamorphosed into cold beasts promising death.

Submerged to his ribs, Lamm took a final glance at the panorama of midtown Manhattan. Panorama of metropolitan panoramas! Manhattan, the sparkling modern-day conjunction of Rome under Caesar and a thousand steel skyscrapers of Babel, alight with its nocturnal glare outshining anything imagined by the ancient sun worshippers of Helios and Apollo. The Williamsburg Bridge glowing its orange trail of tail-lights, the airy floodlit cavity of Ground Zero there like the left lung ripped from Tribeca's fluorescent chest, and on Battery Park's foreshore, hundreds of apartment windows illuminated the passionless blue of TV screens. The residents in those living rooms, staying up late to watch Baghdad burning on CNN, were, of course, oblivious to a hopeless figure sinking into the East River far below their balcony bonsai.

Still, among those apartment windows, Lamm expected – hoped! – to see the silhouette of a face contorted in horror. *Call 911! A man's drowning!* Screams, shrieks, sirens. Then strong hands yanking him to safety; he'd be waterlogged, hypoxic, hypothermic yet breathing. The trouble was, in their living rooms Lamm's potential saviours couldn't hear the gurgled cries of a drowning delinquent above Tom Brokaw's good-gollys blaring from twenty TVs on the same floor. The night owls were too engrossed by the televised shocking and awing of Baghdad, too hypnotized by the green night-vision bombardment of that miserable bulls-eye on the Tigris, to hear Max Lamm screaming through a mouthful of dirty water.

Do you really want to die?

The current tugged him down – so cold! – as toxic mud crumbled underfoot. Lamm was choking, drowning, swept by the backwash of a trash barge chugging two hundred metres downriver. *Go with it. The end.* Spalding Gray did. January 2004: Acclaimed writer, actor Spalding Gray commits suicide by jumping off the Staten Island ferry. His corpse drifted undiscovered for two months. A substantial, respectful obituary in the *New York Times*. In the same body of water, the same time of year. The cruel difference, Lamm instantly recognized, being that until his fatal depression, Spalding Gray was a success. Whereas in a town like New York, the watery demise of a scandalous whoremonger like yourself – a fallen idol known best for your precocious depravity, whose lasting legacy is your disservice to the Jewish people, the war on drugs, American tennis and sportsmanship in general – is unlikely to inspire a dignified obit like Spalding Gray's.

Another reason for killing yourself!

Or a reason against it?

Despite the unchallengeable reasons – the necessity! – for sinking, for swallowing putrid water, for letting go, for letting it happen, Lamm's hands waved above the surface. Should've tied them behind your back. Worse, when his head bobbed up a peculiar sound hollered from his lips. A gargle *and* a scream, unmistakably opposed to his deathly intentions.

Arghhhhh! He-e-lp!

Now somebody else – the sly agent of self-preservation buried within us, appointed to our lives like a judge – was controlling Lamm's limbs the way a hijacker commandeers an aircraft. Unlike the suicidal Saudis responsible for the hole in the skyline nearby, Lamm's hijacker *prevented* the untimely demise. His eyes floated ahead, a ghostly buoy of awareness, and he watched himself screaming, fighting the current, sucking air against the frigid swell. What he could do to stay alive.

Disgraced, decrepit Lamm! How infuriating that liberation in death might be thwarted by some natural impulse, or by fear, or his stubborn stupid attachment to life. But he wasn't surprised. Like Kelly Wesson that week in her Georgetown mansion, staring at Daddy's gun every afternoon yet unable to swallow the barrel and pull her trigger finger, the suicidal resolve was less than concrete.

Is this your survival instinct?

Is it God?

Blurry figures approached on the Battery Park boardwalk.

'He's drowning!'

Shouts, screams, splashes. Amid the glowing apartment blocks, had a silhouette turned off the TV, heard Lamm's cries and called 911? Or a Tribeca yuppie, walking his labradoodle after a late night cooking spreadsheets at Morgan Stanley, had noticed the young outcast drowning a hundred yards off the Battery Park boardwalk? You should've jumped off a thirty-storey ledge. Swan-dived from the deck of the *New York Times* tower. Intentional Death of an Anarchist.

But you want to be rescued.

Putrid mud squashed underfoot, Lamm's head submerged in the East River's chilled thickshake of seawater, stormwater, wastewater and the bubbles of carbon dioxide exiting his blue lips.

It's not too late. Die.

Fragments of shouts piercing the deadly swell. But

whoever it was, they took too long and Lamm kept drowning, perhaps dead already by a coroner's criteria. Down, down, down beneath the warm clear waves that stung his fifteen-year-old nostrils when the swell pitched him into the seabed on Jan Juc beach. His mother on the hot dunes, watching over the rim of a *Harper's Bazaar*, upon her beach towel the wet trove of cockles that he'd combed up from the foam. Deeper, further he'd swim for shells, feeling his creased fingertips along the Bass Strait sandbank, never afraid of biting crabs nor poisonous jellyfish, nor the waves breaking thunderously above, because the beach was a friendly place. *His* place, where the Southern Ocean's translucent wash swept him to shore. Back to his mother, where she sunbaked under the good umbrella she reserved for vacations. Among the phantoms of long-gone summer days, Lamm was dying in Manhattan's moat, cold and grey as a morgue.

He drowned until he was bitten. Not by the small gummy sharks that occasionally spooked Jan Juc's swimmers, nor an errant sea lion if a school of mullet swam uncommonly close to shore. In the East River, it was a fish of five fingers, painfully strong, that chomped his shoulders and pulled him up. Back to the pontoon on the Battery Park foreshore. Lamm's lungs, full of black muck, recoiled as hands compressed his chest.

'*Can you hear me? Breathe!*'

An excruciating force crushing his sternum. Lips – a man's lips – sealing his own. Musty air down his throat.

'*Two . . . four . . . six . . . eight.*'

The weight compressing Lamm's chest. Cold goo hurtling up his trachea. An unendurable pain in his skull.

'*Can you hear me? Wake up!*'

Blackness.

The ambulance roof. Fluorescent tubes buzzing on, off, on. White glare piercing his hypoxic skull. The pain in Lamm's temples! A serrated throb slightly above his ear, at the coronal suture where the frontal and parietal bones fuse. The exact spot where, two years later in London, a beer bottle smashed into a Pakistani teenager's skull.

Hot jagged needles replaced the follicles on Lamm's scalp. A bright white room. Voices, the precise monotone of professional agreement. '*Maintain intubated oxygen . . . note that severe laryngospasm has occurred . . .*' Electronic beeping, a penlight in his pupils, the vital slipperiness of latex fingers invading his throat.

Four days in the coma.

Breakdown.

SEVEN

Endgame. In New York, Lamm threw himself beneath disorder's brakeless train and got dismembered on the tracks. He'd be sodden buried bones, weren't it for a beefcake of a bonds trader with a blonde fashion publicist of a wife, a young Mr and Ms Manhattan, who at 3 a.m. were strolling back to their love nest loft on the Battery Park boardwalk.

The hero – his name was Scott Greer, fresh at Goldman Sachs via Stanford Business School – leapt into the river and freestyled three hundred yards to the drowning stranger. Leapt into the newspapers too; Scott Greer, first the *New York Post*'s man of the week, then interviewed by Barbara Walters under her sugary lights. *Tell me Scott, what does it feel like to be a hero? Are you bothered that you saved a person like Max Lamm?* Later, Greer reappeared on the *Post*'s front page when he received a bravery award from the mayor.

Not to say that Scott Greer, the gallant dreamboat bearing striking resemblance to a young Jimmy Stewart, didn't deserve the adulation. He was New York's newest public hero, whose courage was refreshingly unrelated to the twin towers. The rookie stockbroker who lunged fully clothed into a dark, dangerous current to save a stranger's life. And how ironic, how Kafkaesque – as noted by fossilized columnists in the *New York Times* magazine, by

Hitchens bleary-eyed on the talk show circuit and Larry King straight down the barrel – that Greer, a genuine hero, had rescued a genuine disgrace.

Scott Greer, thirty-four – brains and brawn who served as a young Marine in Kosovo, who wore a flagpin on his lapel, who had, according to rumour, already been approached by aides to Mayor Giuliani – had rescued from the East River the infamous former tennis champ whose primary anaesthetic was the bottle and the cock. The disgraced degenerate who, seven months earlier, had received his own half-page in the *New York Post* sports section for behaviour that, were his punishment meted out by the US Marine Corps and not the Association of Tennis Professionals, would have seen him court-martialled and sentenced to ten years of peeling potatoes in a Navy brig. Possession of illegal narcotics. Solicitation of illegal prostitution. The secretly filmed sex tape that, a week after Lamm's scandal broke, had already logged 805, 000 plays on www.pornotube.com and had since hit three million. You're ejaculating on her tits 115, 000 times a day; no wonder you feel tired. Lamm remained in fourth place on the website's 'most viewed' list:

1. Horny teen lesbians
2. Hot pornstar fuck
3. Amateur anal surprise
4. Max Lamm sex tape
5. Swedish shower blowjob

How many millions of fifteen-year-old boys had stared gape-mouthed at Lamm groaning atop that glistening Salvodorian sculpture of ideal female proportions, at his tongue wrapped lasciviously around her insides like the serpent guarding Eve's apple, and gasped not merely at the masturbatory impulse but the insurmountable pleasures of adulthood incarnate on their laptop screens! Lamm mirrored their adolescent desperation, sucking the call-girl dry like a desert explorer at an oasis. Not for five years, since Lewinsky's testimony to the grand jury, had the quality newspapers reported such useful material for truck drivers alone in the restroom. She *was* hypnotic, this hourglass of a girl pirouetting upon Lamm's cock; slow, wet, engrossing. Her golden body so narrow, she'd break in two if he went any harder. Of course, he never knew he was being filmed.

It often takes a lifetime to become famous through the honourable means – such as painting great paintings, writing literature worth reading, doing innovative science or charitable public works – but three days of a sex scandal makes you better known than most Nobel laureates put together. Thirty years henceforth Lamm would be remembered, at least by tennis aficionados and men in raincoats. Already, millions of internet voyeurs had enjoyed his thirst for that graceful Salvadorian girl; they savoured his desperation, the moist catharsis he pursued unapologetically. Onscreen, Lamm's obvious drive for fucking was temporarily quenched by this Latino whose beauty far exceeded the requirements of her profession, unforgettable for her green eyes and a lilting voice unsuited to the sterility of the Queen's English yet exercising otherworldly power when she cooed in Spanish mid-blowjob.

The disgrace burnt mercilessly, rendering Lamm a charred shell long after his heart and balls had melted in the witch hunt's flames. To the endangered species of upstanding American unswayed by perky young flesh, he was irredeemably abhorrent. Max Lamm, the degenerate slavemaster to a penniless Salvadorian girl, patron to an exploitative pimp, a precociously depraved disappointment who, on the popular online video, spent thirteen mesmerising minutes massaging his prick between her greased breasts.

Lamm's loudest critics – the right-wing radio Rottweilers led by Rush Limbaugh and the Norman Rockwell revivalists at the American Family Association – *loved* tying him to a stake, a quintessentially American stake usually reserved for important men (Bill Clinton, Gary Condit, Gary Hart), then burning him alive on Fox News. Lamm was condemned with editorial vehemence usually reserved for OJ Simpson, the Taliban and the French.

Beneath Hyde Park, Lamm was interred in charcoal and sausage fat, but, he recognized, the burying alive had commenced the year before. In Brooklyn, when the dirt clods were shovelled in by his tormenters. The vicious ringleaders: his conniving doubles partner, Grey Pierce III. His mercenary turncoat of a coach, Sid Einfeld. And once the scandal broke, the popular columnist Anna Cunningham, a rakish blonde Medusa known for her Prada knee-boots and an *ubermenschen* profile that would've made the womanizer Goebbels blush. She'd most recently made news by advocating an electric fence and moat along the Mexican–American border. In a syndicated tirade published by the *Wall Street Journal*, she compared Max Lamm's sexual depravity to Clinton's and his vegetarianism to Hitler's, then she strung him up, condemned his oft-downloaded crimes against womankind, sportsmanship, Reagan's legacy and civilization in general, and cut off his fists and balls with the blunt scalpel named family values. She left Lamm hanging there, a gruesome example to the oversexed Hollywood liberals, so he'd bleed to death from his wrists and amputated dick.

Hopeless, anchorless Lamm! He hadn't seen enough? What Hyde Park's underworld might teach him, he didn't want! He'd suffered the classic creative triptych of depression, alcoholism, attempted suicide. The three-pronged affliction of genius endured by Goya, Van Gogh, Pollock, Francis Bacon, Rothko . . . yet what masterpieces had Lamm painted? He was nothing. Hadn't touched a brush in seven months. The great artists suffered for their art; Lamm's art was to suffer. Disgrace, despair, near-death, banishment . . . that was supposed to lead up the frayed rope ladder of self-improvement, resilience, artistic inspiration . . . not to *this*! Not Lamm's newest worst incarnation: murderer. More than murderer: hate killer, lucrative bounty, white-supremacist bogeyman, psychopathic death-mask.

New York was enough!

Underground, he turned over in his jacket.

Sleep! Please!

Lamm smelt the beer staining his sleeve. Exhibit A: a trace of the murder weapon.

After nightfall, the park's bushes again became living Rorschach blots. Lamm crawled through the scrub without his route muddied by the voices, hallucinations and tremors of sleeplessness. Nevertheless, when he looked into the moonlight's glint or a streetlight's glare, Lamm saw Mr Lewski's ghost rematerialize. A hallucination? A warning of worse to come? He remembered the CCTV cameras, so he wore his hood as the hoodlums do. Pulled over his forehead, a phantom. One of millions.

Lamm felt dizzy from hunger. At the 24-7 convenience store on Great Cumberland Place, he paid £16.65 for three microwaved pumpkin pies, two litres of water, three bananas, two flapjacks, four chocolate bars, a keyring flashlight, a few razors, a toothbrush, toothpaste, batteries, and a £3 Chinese pocket radio imported from a bargain-basement cornucopia by the Yangtze . . . all purchased without a credit card, from his last £50 cash, thereby evading another electronic eye. A fast efficient spree until Lamm glanced at the magazine rack, at the latest edition of the *Evening Standard*.

HATE MURDER TRIGGERS EAST LONDON RACE RIOT

A remarkable headline. A headline that, to Lamm, was no less stunning than the tasers the police used to electrocute the rioters. Beneath the sickening scarlet letters was an unforgettable triptych of three images: a Pakistani grocery engulfed by an arsonist's flames, seven hundred Muslims rallying outside their MP's office, and a bystander's camera-phone photograph of Malik Massawi collapsed on the Camden pavement while the paramedics took his pulse. His body draped in a grey ambulance blanket – a child's blanket, too short for the six foot three inches of this lanky teenage goalie – that left his feet sticking out one end. The boy's white Nike trainers pointing skywards.

Those sneakers spoke to Lamm:

I should be playing football with my friends.

In a photo on page two, the bus shelter was examined by

two forensic investigators wearing white plastic jumpsuits, collecting glass fragments, traces of blood, saliva, hairs. The murderer's genetic cipher was, perhaps, encoiled within a stray strand's innumerable double helixes.

If these people only knew a little about the culprit! That unsensationally, he wasn't an Islamist fanatic deliberately catalysing ethnic discord, nor a bottle-wielding waxwork of Oswald Mosely the aristocratic pre-war fascist. Malik Massawi's killer was merely an exiled Jewish failure pickled in limestone and barbeque grease. A squandered sporting prodigy, wasted scholarly talent, unfulfilled painter, libidinous disgrace, whose insatiable thirst for transgression (until yesterday the central force of his being) had suddenly dissolved like sugar cubes in boiling water.

Lamm stood motionless, staring at the front page. The photos – especially Malik's basketball boots protruding from the body bag – were unforgettably *real*. Obscenely real. Wait until they identify you, until they know that you're a Jew. You'll be on the same accursed page of Jewish infamy as Yitzhak Rabin's assassin and that nutcase Goldstein who attacked the Hebron mosque with a machine gun.

The microwave beeped.

'Today is a bad day,' remarked the man at the register. London's typical convenience store attendant: a skinny moustached guy over from Bangalore to study software engineering.

'The murder, the riot. It is a *very* bad day.'

The microwave beeped again. The attendant's eyebrows arched at his bewildered customer.

'Sir! Your pie is ready!'

Lamm read the front page. Couldn't help himself. These riots he never anticipated! A colossal manhunt? The

PM's condemnation? *That* he expected. The vengeance of Pakistani vigilantes? Terrifying yet unsurprising. The boy was dead, so Lamm predicted his lynch mobs the way a ruined man envisages his bank balance. Of course the tabloids were incendiary. Hysterical, so dangerously sensationalist that Lamm would have agreed to whatever Faustian bargain that Murdoch as Mephistopheles might demand in exchange for averting the journalists' hangman impulses. Give them half a chance, the redtop hacks would re-erect the Tyburn gallows, on the traffic island where two hundred years ago they stood at Marble Arch, and swing Lamm the unconvicted suspect from a noose.

What *was* shocking was the burning drycleaners on Bethnal Green's high street, the BBC van battered by fence posts, the Bangladeshi bystander crushed by a toppled barrier. The proof that what had happened had happened. The East End riots were Britain's most destructive civil disturbance since Saturday 11 April, 1981, when Operation Swamp 81, the Metropolitan Police's clumsy crackdown on black street-crime in Brixton, provoked the night of fiery violence indelibly associated with the hard heel of South London. Brixton had petrol bombs, fire engines trashed, more than 300 police injuries, thirty buildings burned . . . but the East End riots wrought all that *and* one bystander in a coma, another paralysed, East Aldgate on police lockdown and a fifteen-year-old murdered the night before. Had a morsel occupied his stomach, Lamm would've thrown up, right there in the 24-7 convenience store on Great Cumberland Place. Hold it in until you've eaten something.

Next on the rack. Frighteningly on the loose, announced the *Sun* to its four million readers, was a bigoted murderer worthy of the UK's abominable tradition of bigoted murderers. Murderers like the white thugs who stabbed eighteen-year-old Stephen Lawrence, a Jamaican architecture student, at an Eltham bus stop in April 1993. Or the five British-Pakistani hooligans who, on a grey Glasgow afternoon in March 2004, kidnapped a white fifteen-year-old named Kriss Donald, took him on a 200 mile joyride, and then, in a deserted walkway near the Celtic Football Club, stabbed the boy thirteen times, doused him in petrol, set him alight and left him to die. Or the London Nailbomber, a deranged neo-Nazi named David Copeland, who in 1999 planted homemade bombs at a supermarket on Brixton's Electric Avenue (to kill blacks), on Brick Lane (to kill Muslims) and in a pub on Soho's Old Compton Street (to kill gays). Or the Gay Slayer, Colin Ireland, who strangled five men mid-coitus following his 1993 New Year's resolution to become a serial killer.

Britain's despised, deranged criminals recently joined – in publicity if not intention – by the Racist Camden Killer, and look at how we'll catch *that* bastard! Lamm ticked off the ways on his cold fingers; one little piggy's the forensic pathologists, two little piggies is the DNA analysis, three little piggies is the elite Homicide Command Unit at New Scotland Yard, four little piggies is the £10,000 public reward for information leading to the culprit's arrest . . . in a few minutes he ran out of fingers.

Already on the steps of Number 10, the prime minister had vowed to catch the murderer, showcasing the same tight-lipped, little-eyed affectation of tragedy that did wonders for him in the days following Princess Di's demise. And after the mandatory intermission for topless Lucy the

Lovely Lass on page three of the *Sun*, worse news awaited on page four:

> Mr Paul Fedorcio, the Metropolitan Police spokesman, confirmed that several British-Muslim vigilante gangs are attempting to avenge Mr Massawi's murder. Mr Fedorcio urged Muslim communities not to 'take the law into their own hands'.

Your death sentence. Has the Ayatollah pronounced a *fatwa*? If so, Lamm wouldn't expect a cheer squad the calibre of Rushdie's − PEN International, N Mailer, M Kundera, S Sontag, E L Doctorow − to lobby the Iranian foreign ministry on his behalf. Grumpy hairy Khomeini sentenced Salman Rushdie to death, but *that* apostate is a famous writer. He's written quality novels that some people in the street have heard of. No small achievement. Whereas beneath an extinct Hyde Park barbeque hides a carnal disgrace. A libidinous exile from America *and* Australia, guilty of murder unless the jury believes it was self-defence. Which it was and they wouldn't. The lack of intention doesn't abrogate the crime.

Munching two hot pumpkin pies beneath the warm pipes, Lamm read the newspapers in the spill of his Chinese flashlight. He would keep these front pages, for the same reason that some cancer survivors want their tumours preserved in a jar. To credulous, irreprehensible readers out there in ordinaryland, to the non-murderers of Britain, the headlines *were* terrifying. RACIST RIOT MURDERER ON THE LOOSE. What right-minded parent wouldn't fear that? HATE KILLER STALKS NORTH LONDON. Max Lamm: the capital's reincarnated combo of Heinrich Himmler, Andre the Giant and the villain who assassinated Archduke Franz Ferdinand and triggered World War I.

The LA riots were worse, Lamm told himself. Correct. Over four days in central Los Angeles during late April 1992, there were fifty-three casualties, two thousand injuries and nearly a thousand buildings destroyed. But those white cops didn't kill Rodney King.

EIGHT

Friday 8 April

Already Lamm wore the timeless *shmutz of* the vagrant. Hair matted with oil, dust, charcoal. Blackened fingernails. Dirt encrusted his one set of clothes: the maroon rain jacket that saw his worst moments in New York (including the East River's frigid depths); a woollen Navy jumper purchased for ten pounds at an army surplus shop in the Camden Market; black Levi's too damp to keep his legs warm; Hexalite tennis shoes courtesy of the Reebok sponsorship that ceased the day his dick made the *New York Times* sports pages.

Everything else that Lamm owned in London remained at his mouldy flat in Golders Green. Where for a year termites had devoured the rotting mantelpiece in the living room, spiralling from their pinprick holes to fascinate him when he awoke at 3 p.m. on a wine-stained mattress. The last bottle of cheap red empty, translucent dribble speckling the oily pillow because that month's roommate had charitably rotated Lamm's head so he wouldn't choke on his own vomit. If the police had identified the suspect, they'd be watching that address.

The newspapers reported that the investigation was

'making rapid progress', but Scotland Yard hadn't matched a name to the faceless culprit in the surveillance footage. So Max Lamm's personal notoriety, if he was to be remembered by anybody for anything, remained in his youth as a tennis champ. Before London, before the East River, Lamm was notable for his adolescence as a tennis prodigy, his native athleticism, his squandered ambition, his remarkable tenacity on the tennis court, in the art studio and the classroom . . . though like most people who are good at everything, ultimately he excelled at nothing.

His extended family, schoolteachers, classmates, the sniping parents of teenage tennis rivals, for years they talked up the same thing: Max Lamm's *potential*. Celebrated on the way up, notorious on the way down. Only after the fall did those people really enjoy discussing Lamm, the vanquished hotshot. The tennis champ, captain of the soccer team, A-grade essayist, gifted painter, best speaker in the debating club, who was reassuringly revealed as an oversexed degenerate whoremonger. A fool depraved beyond his years, who judging from the two-minute video clip that got the search engines chugging in March 2003, felt most alive fucking a Salvadorian call-girl in an illegal whorehouse on Second Avenue. A bag of contraband white powder visible on the bedside table.

The warm buzz of *schadenfreude*! To see a talented young man climb the precarious rope up to something stupendous, then snatch away the safety net as he falls. And don't forget, the critics added, that Max Lamm's a hater of women! A spectacular misogynist, Norman Mailer without the unquenchable literary fire and the ex-wife stabbed. Lamm who hates people as a species, who hates love, laughter, decency, celebration and solid unspectacular achievement.

The chauvinist pig Lamm who hates hugs, kisses and family values, who hates walks on the beach, picnics in the park, baby photos in the wallet, *shabbos* dinner with his parents. Ultimately, his critics agreed, the ghoul hates himself.

'Your boy hates what we love. *That's* what he loves,' Lou Schiff, the esteemed plastic surgeon and president of Mizrachi synagogue, told Lamm's father at the kosher bakery the week the scandal broke.

'The kid loves to hate. But really he hates himself.'

Schiff walked away to untie his schnauzer, without saying goodbye. The kid's like that for a reason, they all agreed. It's the parents' fault too.

Lamm's spring of talent, once irrepressibly bubbling at his core, dried over in the summer of 2004. When *everybody* – hairdressers in Sydney, cod fisherman in Newfoundland, forklift drivers in rural Ohio – learnt about the girl from El Salvador and the video that she 'accidentally' left in the lobby of the Howard Johnson's Hotel on Second Avenue. The sex tape she swore that she never knew existed.

A half-page exclusive in the *New York Post*, a two-minute story at the end of the ESPN sports bulletin, and within a day, Lamm made the network news. Followed by his meltdown in the first round of the US Open, near-suicide in the East River; *everything*. In the *New York Times* sports section for three days straight, on the front pages in Australia. The silver lining: across three continents, Max Lamm inspired responsible parents to lecture their cumstruck adolescents about how not to sabotage their life's prospects.

By August, Lamm was popular not only among the porno search engines, but in the 'Jews in Sports' database of Jew-Watch.com, the popular anti-Semitic bulletin board run by a crank Aryan-supremacist librarian from Missouri. A venal website, ranked number one on Google's search results for 'Jew', that claims that the blood of Christian children softens the Passover matzah; that denies the pogroms, ghettos and gas chambers; that portrays the Nazi hatemonger Julius Streicher as a blameless victim of Zionist bloodlust at Nuremburg.

'Max Lamm,' somebody called Panzer72 wrote on the bulletin board, 'demonstrates the dishonesty and depravity that is second nature to the Jew.' Unbound on the internet, Lamm's mistake became a vicious tearaway beast, like the savage Alsatian that Issl Koch, the camp commandant's monster of a wife at Buchenwald, let loose on terrified Jewish children.

And not just the anonymous anti-Semites on the Jew-Watch chatroom. United in their zealous multitudes were evangelicals against Max Lamm; America's creepily polite family values fanatics who, like the Saudi terrorists they despise even more than the Clintons, value fanaticism over family. The loyal evangelicals, fifty million strong from Alabama to Anchorage, who bombarded Reebok's headquarters with approximately seventeen thousand emails and four thousand phone messages demanding that Lamm, the amoral libidinous disgrace, disappear from the firm's endorsement program or else America's conservative Christians would unanimously choose another brand of running shoe.

How these evangelicals abhorred the fallen champ and his ilk! Because decadent Jews like Max Lamm, the beneficiaries of a global financial conspiracy led by Soros, Geffen, Spielberg, Art Garfunkle and the other wealthy Jewish liberals, diluted the megachurches' illusionary re-creation of

Eisenhower's golden age. Making their mark that election year, Falwell's followers yearned for the vanquished era of safe segregated streets, of creationism in science classrooms, of white churchgoing values unshattered by *Roe v Wade* or the *Brown* decision, of incorruptible small government and priests who never fall for the temptation of the altar boy's flesh, of an apple-pie America that never existed anyway outside of Frank Capra movies and Norman Rockwell paintings on the cover of the *Saturday Evening Post*.

The family values lobby successfully petitioned the Association of Tennis Professionals to suspend Max Lamm from future tournaments. His career – fourteen years of training, six hours a day – dissolved by the conservative coalition of fat cat Falwell, the megalomaniacal psychologist James Dobson of Focus on the Family, and right-wing titan Ralph Reed (a few months before he was exposed for helping the crooked lobbyist Jack Abramoff fleece $82 million from a Native American tribe in Mississippi).

So ignore the so-called news in that leftist cumrag the *New York Times*! Ignore Bin Laden and his lieutenants brainstorming in a cave in northern Pakistan, or the Jordanian kid in a suicide belt who killed thirty people yesterday at a fruit market in the Sunni Triangle. Ignore the glaciers melting into slurpee slush, ignore all the news since Satan stuck a cigar up his intern, because finally, here was something for the evangelicals to really get worked up about!

Max Lamm's sex-tape spectacle was a red rag to those who pray for the resurrected reign of Ronald the Great Communicator; the millions of Americans with flagpoles stuck in their yard and up their spine, who yearn for the early 1980s when the president was hewn from Mount

Rushmore's craggy rock, thought like a rock, and unlike the shadowy terrorists arriving on student visas from Saudi Arabia, the USA's most dangerous enemy was big, red and smack bang in the middle of the world map. Back when the enemy was like us and didn't want to die.

For a week the born-agains overloaded the switchboards at Reebok and the Association of Tennis Professionals. They phoned the Midwestern newsrooms of NBC, ABC, CBS. 'Get that disgusting sex freak and his Mexican prostitute *off* my TV set!' Not enough to change the channel, the drug-addled whoremonger of a tennis champ must *disappear*. Rush Limbaugh's soccer-mom storm troopers hadn't been as disgusted by a sports story since Janet Jackson flashed her pierced nipple at the Superbowl and revealed to America's children that tits exist. Lamm was disappointed that when the newspapers featured images from his video, the prostitute's spectacular natural breasts were blurred by pixelated circles. They show Saddam hanging on a rope, but a nipple – the most divine you've ever sucked – is too abhorrent? The kids should read about you in the Swedish papers.

For America's stressed-out mums at the grocery checkout, Lamm was ten minutes' diversion from the exhausting world. On the rack alongside M&Ms and Snickers, besmirched in the *National Enquirer*, he was a welcome distraction from their defaulting home loan, rocketing petrol prices, the body bags back from Baghdad or Kabul, this month's corporate fat cat scandal with ten thousand jobs axed, another misfit shooting his classmates at junior high in Arkansas, the three little monsters in the back seat screaming they want McDonald's . . .

Meet Max Lamm's downtrodden jury. They condemned

him at hairdressers and truckstop diners, at train stations, bus stops and hospital waiting rooms where they waited for a diagnosis too expensive to cure. In a hundred thousand supermarket checkout lines in a thousand dead-end towns in a hundred depressed counties where the manufacturing machines were unbolted from the factory floor and shipped to China, Max Lamm's sex scandal helped ordinary Americans to feel good about themselves. Their indispensible consolation: at least I'm not *that* stupid.

September 2004: While Kelly Wesson cut the letters KMD (Kelly Must Die) into her left arm in a Washington mansion, Lamm planned his own death. The desire-not-to-exist, the timeless escape that feels natural as bleeding to a victim of the insurmountable. Now go drown in the East River. The closing act of your descent. The descent set in motion by your thirst for transgression – for *her*, the whorehouse's otherworldly new girl fresh off the bus from El Salvador – that ripples through your marrow.

Yes, Max Lamm knew Goya's naked human impulses: *fight*, *flee*, *fuck*. They'd engorged him, overpowered his better judgement, but until then London never killed anyone. Never provoked a race riot or a prime minister's condemnation.

So, Lamm realized on his first morning beneath Hyde Park, despite the dissolution of all he'd ever worked for, despite the undiluted catastrophe of his life, he had, nevertheless, progressed at something. At fucking up. His preponderance for disaster was effortless, inartificial, irreducible. Who'd put it there? Why? Incomprehensible. Incomprehensible as nine months of hell in the National Guard seemed to Kelly Wesson.

One day you wake up and all you know is incoherence.

* * *

Aaron Krickstein. An unwieldy name, brandishing its Jewishness like an oversized racquet. Krickstein, the Michigan-born tennis pro who, at the 1995 Australian Open, shocked the pundits by reaching the semifinals to challenge Andre Agassi. Their showdown took four hours on an afternoon freakishly wet even for a climate intemperate as Melbourne's. Beneath the arena a water main burst, stopping play for ninety minutes as ball boys dried the court with hand pumps and squeegee mops. Aaron Krickstein was a rare Jewish specimen of beefy athletic prowess (reassuringly encumbered by a big nose and a Chassidic rabbi's eyebrows) whose grand-slam heroics inspired sixteen-year-old Max Lamm. At the Maccabi tennis club he trained every day except Saturday when, owing to rabbinical pressure, the Caulfield Park courts were rented instead to a *goyische* booking from the local Girl Guides chapter.

Lamm never yearned for grand-slam victories, his likeness on billboards, a swollen Swiss bank account . . . the fairytale prayed for by obsessed tennis parents in tracksuits, themselves champs twenty years ago behind the Iron Curtain, who sat courtside at junior tournaments to cheer their prepubescent progeny – Sacha, Yevgeny, Mirko, Radovan, et al – and hurl abuse at the opponent's parents. When ethnic grievances were present – a Serbian kid playing a Croatian, or a Macedonian against a Greek – sometimes a brawl erupted on court, the parents hurling chairs and yelling insults in a language their children barely understood.

Yet Lamm cared for nothing but the endorphin rush, the happy ache in his muscles regardless of whether he won or lost. The satisfaction endowed by this sport that he was strangely, naturally good at. Three hours' training today, three hours tomorrow, an under 16s tournament on Sunday, and he enjoyed it, even the morning drill – *jog right, left, right, left, forehand, backhand* – that afterwards bestowed a blanket of relaxation rivalled only by his other two favourite pastimes: reading dusty books that he recovered from an old cabinet in the basement, the classic adventure novels his father had read as a boy – *The Sword in the Stone, My Glorious Brothers, Twenty Thousand Leagues Under the Sea, Journey to the Center of the Earth* – and the brief post-ejaculatory calm before Lamm wondered if, despite the car's absence from the driveway, his father had been watching through the skylight or the heating grill and knew where his son hid the pirated porno videos that he purchased at school for ten dollars a pop from the notorious Marty Weinberg.

At the Maccabi tennis club, Lamm's talent – his *potential* – was unmistakable. An unexpected, generous force, reinforced every time this gangly libidinous rake trounced another opponent in straight sets. His talent in full bloom on 28 January, 1995. The day Lamm's father, Mel, ran from his Caulfield chiropractic office despite a half-full waiting room, drove six blocks to the courts and interrupted afternoon training. In front of the other boys – Friedman with the lisp and a one hundred and eighty kilometres per hour serve, Millstein the developer's son with a backyard court and always the new equipment, Blashki who once took an ace in the groin and had to see a dick doctor – Mel Lamm shook his son like a dud ball.

'Max! Did you hear the news? He did it! Krickstein's playing Agassi in the semis!'

The under-16s threw their racquets skywards, cheering

not for the political symbolism of a Jewish underdog challenging the Las Vegan superstar of Iranian heritage, but for the rare spectacle of a Jew succeeding at *any* sport. Krickstein, who'd beaten Stefan Edberg days before, was only two matches away from winning a grand slam tournament – he could be the first Jewish player to do so – without assistance from the usual Yiddish brigade of lawyers, doctors, accountants and haberdashers. Later at the clubhouse, the coach and some of the parents treated the boys to kosher pizza and ice cream as they watched Krickstein's big match live on TV.

According to the *Australian Jewish News*, that night similar gatherings occurred in Jewish neighbourhoods from Bondi Junction to Williamsburg, Monsey to Beverly Hills, London's Golders Green to kibbutzes with satellite dishes, as Jews worldwide came together to cheer their man. It was a bizarre showdown, unforgettable for when the arena's drainage system malfunctioned and a geyser erupted on court. Nevertheless, Krickstein returned to his Jewish roots and lost the match 4-6, 4-6, 0-3, defaulting with an injured hamstring.

Adam Millstein's father screamed at the TV screen.

'Krickstein could have won the first set! The hopeless schmuck should've stayed in college!'

The following night at the kitchen table. Lamplight reflected off Mel Lamm's bald scalp. Silence. The father stared into his son's eyes.

'Max, somebody *brilliant* sent this to me.'

A glossy brochure lay unfolded on the linoleum tabletop. But after a tiring four hours' training, Lamm's interest wasn't forthcoming.

'See the guy in the photo?' Lamm's father pushed the brochure across the table. 'That's Aaron Krickstein's coach. Krickstein's *personal* coach.

'His name's Sid Einfeld, and he's helped twenty-three players break the top ten. He's among the best coaches in the United States. Arguably *the* best.'

The brochure's centrepiece, in soft focus like an advertisement for cheap jewellery, was a brownstone clubhouse flying the Stars and Stripes above eight hard courts on a fine spring day.

'Sid Einfeld's got a tennis academy up near Albany in New York State. It's a reasonable train ride from my cousin in Williamsburg. Remember Leo Chrapot?'

Atop the coach's photo, his title in golden block letters:

Expert Trainer, Motivator and Biomechanical Therapist, Sid J Einfeld.

The Strategic Mastermind Behind Twelve Grand Slam Titles. Sid Einfeld is – here the letters swelled into sixteen-point font – THE MAN WHO COACHES THE COACHES.

Einfeld's toothy grin said *look what I've done!* and *let me do it for you!* A tanned rake, about sixty but fitter than most men half his age, distinctive for the white shag sprouting like alfalfa from his tennis shirt and an uncanny resemblance to Tony Bennett.

'Son, I have wonderful news. Sid was down here with Krickstein and he scouted at the juniors. Last week he saw you beat that Swedish kid. Today he called me. He's gonna wait until you grow a little taller, then he wants to work with you!'

Three days after his eighteenth birthday, when Lamm relocated to his cousin's house in Williamsburg, Brooklyn, he had won another four junior tournaments, signed a sponsorship deal with Reebok and bade his relatives farewell during dinner at Sophia's, an aircraft hangar of an Italian bistro specializing in sentimental marathons of duplicated presents and shrieking babies. For three hours that Thursday evening, his extended family – the Lamms, the Chrapots, the Snyders – unanimously proclaimed that their young hotshot Max was destined for something stupendous. His father toasted a *l'chaim*, predicting that his boy's achievements would confer *nachas* not only upon their clan, nor the Maccabi tennis club that nourished his talent, but upon the Jewish people as the chosen nation.

The messianic expectations for his new coach yet to be confirmed, three days later Lamm arrived at Penn station. Leo Chrapot was waiting by the baggage carousel and immediately Lamm warmed to his cousin, a computer analyst of characteristic girth, who stuffed the suitcases into his Hyundai mini, said to hell with the traffic and went for a scenic drive over the Brooklyn Bridge, for burgers on Bedford Avenue and finally to Lamm's basement bedroom beneath their Williamsburg brownstone.

Four days a week Lamm rode the Amtrak up to Sid Einfeld's academy. His maiden semester of relentless drills, militaristic coaching, gifted hitting partners and, most satisfyingly, improvement in his game. After two months, he beat a Belarusian kid ranked in the ATP Top 100. Max Lamm possessed the same brash talent that, Coach Einfeld remarked, he'd noticed thirty years earlier in a cocksure rookie named John McEnroe. For the next five years, Lamm stayed at the academy for three months every year and New York City – for a hundred and fifty years the world's premier maternity ward for outrageous dreams – suggested that Lamm's father was right. Everything would work out. It *had* to.

After Lamm's initial excursions to the gargantuan galleries in the city, he came to know Williamsburg; the best and worst of Bedford Avenue's junk shops, bookstores, bagelries, art spaces, $5 barbers. An internet café-cum-laundromat run by a Lubavitcher in a black hat, long beard and *payes*, who turned a blind eye to the thirteen-year-old kids in the corner gawking at playboy.com. The dull clack of the L train, the frigid grey lap of the East River chilling Lamm's basement window when the wind turned. Atlantic Avenue crowded at lunchtime with hungry clerks from City Hall, black kids in gigantic white T-shirts milling outside the movie theatre, Korean street sweepers in lime-green overalls, Puerto Rican grocers yelling through mouthfuls of plantains, art school students wearing Ray-Bans, black jeans and Cuban heels, arguing the merits of *Mapplethorpe v Basquiat* as they walked to their how-to-rip-off-Warhol class at Brooklyn Art College. It became thuddingly familiar as the midtown skyline lost its postcard novelty. You can leave Manhattan for the tourists and the rats.

Yet, though invariably denied by the parents of a talented child, expectations for success never rest on sturdy ground. As Lamm recalled a year later beneath a barbeque, during the summer of 2003 his predisposition for catastrophe – that talent more irrepressible, more *him*, than the dexterity with a racquet or paintbrush – finally concluded its terrible gestation. His force of self-destruction, emerging like a maladaptive butterfly from a poisoned cocoon. It began on the Saturday evening that should have been a celebration, because Lamm had won a wildcard singles entry into the US Open.

For Lamm's envious doubles partner, that weekend became a different, reprehensible kind of celebration. He was Gray Pierce III, the Ohio State college champ who accrued sour satisfaction from taking Lamm to the beginning of the end. The freckled scion of a Cleveland military dynasty, his father ashamed that their firstborn had ditched the Marines for an effeminate pursuit like tennis, Gray Pierce was jealous of Lamm's US Open berth. A six-foot-four goliath with a killer forehand and an ironing board's posture, Pierce was convinced that his partner was stealing the credit for their five straight victories. As Lamm discovered, Gray Pierce's stiff back concealed a sharp stake way, way up his arse; a stake that the sunburnt Midwestern Judas used to crucify his doubles partner that weekend in Manhattan.

That Saturday evening, fifteen of the Matchpoint Academy's recruits visited the city to celebrate the twenty-first birthday of Josip Zelic, a Croatian who was runner-up at the junior French Open. At Lit, a labyrinthine bar beneath Second Avenue, they guzzled Belgian beer, vodka and donuts in lieu of a birthday cake. As midnight tolled, Gray Pierce stumbled outside to find a cash machine. He staggered drunk down the street and, by undeserved serendipity for the carrot-topped snitch, spied his doubles partner outside the Howard Johnson's Hotel at East Eighth Street.

There was Max Lamm, discretely passing $200 cash to the girl from El Salvador. Her chocolate silhouette unmistakable in a red stretch dress and scarlet stilettos to her knees. The girl's businesslike nonchalance, her obliviousness to Lamm's artless kiss goodbye, indicated her venerable profession more explicitly than the outfit. Uncannily, she resembled

Gabriela Sabatini, the retired Argentine bombshell of tennis who has a pink rose named in her honour. Naturally for a natural son of a bitch, Gray Pierce filmed the encounter on his camera phone, that product of Japan offering the kind of peer-to-peer surveillance that would have made J Edgar Hoover hard beneath his silk panties.

Lamm's descent begins.

NINE

Lagaya. He never remembered her full name, only its length (a three-worder long even for Spanish) requiring the throaty '*chhh*' sound (splattering phlegm during correct pronunciation) that's essential to the language. If she'd grown up in the USA, not in a slum in a dictatorship best known for bananas and death squads, Lagaya would have likely graced Manhattan's catwalks as a clotheshorse. Her gangly trunk, humankind's closest incarnation to the gazelle, hadn't thickened in the four years since she was sixteen years old. Small-breasted for the girls at 738 Second Avenue, yet, owing to her face – naturally shiny like Aragonese Spanish honey, perfectly symmetrical, a radiant never-seen muse for Manhattan's dead gay aficionados of beauty like Warhol, Jean-Michel Basquiat, Robert Mapplethorpe – she was the second-most requested hooker at the whorehouse, behind Rosanna whose watermelon-sized double-D cups would, had the surgery occurred in the US and not Tijuana, cost four-thousand dollars a tit.

The pimp, Carlos, was surprised that old-fashioned beauty ran a close second in demand to Manhattan's tightest tit-fuck. But no mystery to her men. Lagaya was hypnotic, beguiling for the languid, unforced grace that her clients didn't deserve. Her captivating glow – the bewitching vitality animating the angular chin, shadowy cheekbones, cascading brown locks – had yet to be drained by wayward kids, domestic violence, street drugs, psychopathic clients, forced eviction, abusive pimps . . . the usual hindrances plaguing women forced into her profession. Her cherubic radiance – a genetic trait observed in the glossy scarlet-cheeked faces of native Central Americans like her father back in San Salvador – belied the dull beige featurelessness of her prison, a third-floor hotel suite, where she was made to fuck five nights a week.

If Lagaya only knew it, her cheekbones would have landed her a gig at a classy no-name joint uptown, an establishment servicing Wall Street brokers, big-shot CEOs, stressed surgeons; the high-tipping clientele who tell their wives they're working late, drink a martini at the Council on Foreign Relations, then take their girl to a room at the Hilton booked under a fake name. But the pimp, a brutal Dominican named Carlos Brenes, never mentioned the money that Lagaya was missing. Nobody did; not the other Latin girls just as uninformed about the Manhattan market-place, not her cumhappy clients enjoying the bargain. Lagaya was too young, too poor, too exquisitely chiselled, too easily deceived owing to her illiteracy in English, for Midtown's foremost illegal whorehouse to squander. Of the thirty-seven Salvadoran, Honduran or Guatemalan women enslaved there, it was she that Carlos – himself a once-penniless illegal immigrant who'd mastered the cruel pragmatism essential for success in America's blackmarket – guarded most closely.

One appointment, Lamm too was hooked. Exceptional

pleasure stripped of its exceptional attachments. His first time as a payer (and only his fifth time ever), he was nervous, half-ashamed, ravenous. In his father's old books in the basement – the dusty leather-bound editions of Bernard Shaw, Hemingway and Fitzgerald, or George Orwell's accounts of skid row in pre-war Paris and London – the prostitutes came in two types: unfortunate victims of happenstance who get rehabilitated by gentlemen widowers, or canny strumpets for whom the emotionless monotony of fucking long ago sapped any humanlike impulse. Lagaya was neither. She was addictively *real*.

Amid her physical poise, Lamm noticed the solitary blemish; a serpentine birthmark, curved like a scythe, blackening the coffee base of her spine until it disappeared into her minature arse. Like a dotless question mark, oscillating as Lamm went at her from behind. Not an unconcealable juggernaut like Gorbachev's – hers merely a dark streak the length of a few matchsticks – but that birthmark mocked Lamm, jeered at his irresponsible libidinous excesses, just as they and he were coming to fruition. By introducing the hint of imperfection into their trysts – the hint, therefore, of reality and his exploitative recklessness – that birthmark marred his pleasure. But she was too good to give up.

Hopeless, horny Lamm! Sometimes couldn't find his rhythm, couldn't finish up, until he gazed not at Lagaya's golden hips and that birthmark, but her neck glistening with sweat, sticky with tangled hair, as she moaned convincingly into the pillow.

'You're a good one,' she cooed afterwards. Had the bastard of a pimp taught her to say that? Then she gulped a shot of decent Scotch whisky, a gift from a periodontist client who, she recounted, was so paranoid about hygiene that he'd jerk off wearing a condom to keep his hands from getting dirty.

Lamm always used the hotel's back entrance. According to a client that he met in the lobby, the big danger was the private investigators camped across the street, waiting to shoot the incriminating photo for a jilted rich wife. Up in the room, they started with small talk. Lagaya asking what he liked, setting the timer, riding him until the disabling climax. Lamm's ingenuity: soliciting so many dreamlike positions in so short a time.

Of course they didn't kiss. The working girl's unofficial code of practice. It took four appointments until, in a disorientated, dehydrated instant, Lagaya permitted an impulsive peck as she felt the rare, rare seed of an orgasm stir yet swiftly subside. Barely ten seconds, yet as their lips intertwined she didn't push him away. She wanted it. This inhalation of animal intimacy, born of misshapen mutual desire, piercing her humdrum schedule of commercial copulation. In Max Lamm's vulnerability, his pathetic infatuation, did she see a way out? This was Lagaya's first moment of pleasure since she arrived in New York and the sexual act became as unremarkable as touching your nose. As Lamm departed into the corridor, she called out.

'Wait!' she yelled from the sofa, halfway through rolling a joint. 'I no kiss client. Okay? Big mistake.'

At the elevator Lamm paused, in case she added anything more. The corridor silent but for the rattle of trucks on Broadway and, down the hall, infrequent groans from a client visiting the Guatemalan lady with removable teeth, which was apparently her drawcard. The door ajar, Lamm peeked back into Lagaya's room. On the couch, the joint unravelled in her lap, she gazed deep in thought at the venetians pierced by dirty sunlight.

Wednesdays approached; she intoxicated him. His disgraceful, delicious indulgence. Lagaya's clinical availability reduced a modern man's striving – the obsession with a good job, flat abs, a nice car, sparkling conversation, the right moment to kiss her, the tactful invitation back to his apartment – to the elaborate sham that it is. On the tennis court, in the locker room, in the gym, the lecture theatre or awake alone in bed, she was everywhere. Her glossy angular face, her tiny hands, her arresting vernacular of shantytown Spanish and the streetwise jibes she learnt from reruns of *Law and Order*. The taut golden bridge of skin he licked, between her perineum and the cleft of her arse, that mystifyingly remained unsullied despite three or four clients a day. Lagaya's narrow brown body beneath him, bare. Compulsively, addictively, deliciously, she justified to Lamm the Western world's limitless preoccupation with sex. But it wasn't just the sex; he was fascinated by her past too. The horrific adolescence in El Salvador that she wouldn't – *couldn't?* – describe to him.

Ferocious lust and sufficient ignorance to facilitate the mystery. Is love, in its embryonic stages, ever anything more?

Sentimental, reckless Lamm! If the four horsewomen of the apocalypse – Hilary, Oprah, Condoleezza and Maggie Thatcher – galloped into that brothel, mid-coitus, to amputate his dick live on the *NBC Today* show, he wouldn't have objected in theory. He knew he'd lost control. The animal desire tramples your better judgement like a jackboot upon a weed. At first Lagaya's aquiline body was enough, her moist obsequiousness rented at reasonable

87

rates. Their unspoken agreement that she'd do anything up to the mildly depraved. The looks she shot him mid-blowjob, perhaps copied from a French porno at the pimp's orders. And her lingerie! Straps, hooks, bras, garter belts, corsets. Sheer panties of a quality incongruous for this shitty hotel. Silk hosiery in three shades of cream, knickers in satin, chiffon, lace. A fancy bra, a good Dior fake so tight it embossed swirling flowers upon her nipples. The textures, fabrics, fits, transparencies . . . so bewitching!

Max Lamm: a dirty old man before his time. The way the panties embraced her explicit hipbones, the extras she wore to turn him on like a bar heater. Red silk thongs shrinking inside her. G-strings so thin they twanged like a slack double bass. Bustiers; their exciting contrast against her tight roasted skin. Push-up bras ramming her small breasts neckwards, so accentuating their circumference that sometimes he wouldn't unhook the hook. Couldn't predict the colour! Burgundy red. Creamy white. Navy blue. Sometimes she wore a teddy of all three; how patriotic. Who else in her hometown of San Salvador, apart from the mistresses of the generals, possesses fancy tricolour underwear like that?

Despite her star-spangled tits, the immigration department wants her deported. *Injusticia!* With two other girls from San Salvador, Lagaya was locked into an unrefrigerated truck smuggling counterfeit DVD players across the hottest, driest, shittiest part of the US–Mexican border between Nuevo Progreso, Tamaulipas and Progreso Lakes, Texas. Three hours down a dirt track two hundred miles north of the Rio Grande, the fat driver with a scarred right cheek – she never learnt his name – orders the girls to get out. They wait in the heat, near a ransacked trailer rusting in the organ cactus and Mexican feather grass. *Desperado!* The girls weep. Stranded, forgotten, they'll die of thirst. *Nuestro lecho de muerte* – it's our deathbed!

Four hours later, a battered Toyota van trundles through the sagebrush against the unbroken blue horizon. *Salvation!* The mules – two Coahuila cowpokes who can't be older than twenty – lock the girls in the back. They get three bottles of water, two loaves of hard bread, a few brown bananas. Occasionally they stop on a deserted stretch, so the cargo can pee in a bush. Three days later, the girls are delivered to the Manhattan whorehouse.

Lagaya gets an hour's rest in a spare suite. Then Carlos inspects her, barking in Spanish; her lack of English is an asset in this line of work. He demands a blowjob, and the pig of a pimp groans agreeably. She's allowed to make a phone call (if Carlos dials the number and listens in). She calls the youngest of her three sisters in San Salvador. Tell mother I've got a job as a *ninera* – a nanny. She will be so pleased! When the money starts coming in, her father will get his medication. Antibiotics for the tuberculosis, and the Inderal beta blockers – at US$55 a pack – to alleviate his heart condition. Lagaya's sisters know that she's pleasuring fat crooks for fifteen dollars a day, but they promise not to tell *padre*.

This was Lagaya Aranxta Marguelis's escape from the slash and burnt slums of San Salvador, where the death squads of the Alianza Republicana Nacionalista murdered peasants, dissidents, missionaries, nuns, children. *Her* slum, where three thousand *gauchos* share a pit for a sewer, wide as an Olympic pool, sometimes a bloated pig or dog rotting in the middle. Eight years ago, Lagaya's kid brother Miguel scratched his forearm on a mess of chicken wire protruding from that cesspool. It didn't hurt, he thought nothing of it and twelve days later he was dead from septicaemia. Her uncle Pedro disappeared one evening in 1981; his body was never recovered. But nobody was surprised, because a month earlier he'd shown mass graves to a *Newsweek* journalist who'd arrived after government soldiers raped and murdered Jean Donovan, a Catholic nun from Connecticut. A girl like Lagaya had a choice: get out or face the Torquemada gangs armed with machetes and M16s left over from the war. Those teenage thugs who graduated from petty robbery to the cocaine routes, who raped three of her friends and shot her neighbour Ronaldo dead because he wouldn't give them a pack of cigarettes.

A few blocks uptown from her brothel, the Lagayas of New York – tanned and skinny as she, yet the product of childhoods a universe apart – yabber over organic kiwi juice and seaweed salad. Esssential rations for these shiny young things toting Jackie O's big sunglasses and nasal voices of undiluted vacuity. Their manicures unblemished despite the sushi at Nobu or last night's handjob for the new guy at Goldman Sachs. It's lunchbreak from sub-editing a fashion mag or kissing ass at a PR firm, and time to discuss when Mr Perfect's gonna pop the question, or the bitch of a receptionist over at *Vogue*, or this season's hots and nots, or the new books they purchased for their summer reading up at the Hamptons: the latest 700-page bestseller about a geisha and the collected works of D Brown, C Bushnell, Dr Phil and the Ya Ya Sisterhood.

Meanwhile with her mouth Lagaya sucks pearly aggression out of Carlos the pimp's buddies. She resists the urge to teach the bastards a lesson, to take a bite so the blood and Viagra flow. She calms these stupefyingly hairy

Latino criminals from the Bronx, disassociating herself from her own skin as they grope, grip, groan, defiling beauty they neither deserve nor understand. She imagines that she is swimming, in a jungle lagoon that she once saw in a 1970s tourist brochure about El Salvador. As the clients ram her face into the mattress, she tells herself to dive – *Nadar! Nadar!* – and marvels at the warm clear water bubbling off the sand bed. The clients leave a tip, then return to their bored wives and screaming kids, where, sated for another week, they don't get so horny that they'll shoot a guy dead during a poker game.

Indirectly, Lagaya's preventing murders. For that she – and throughout the five boroughs ten thousand Latin American sex slaves like her – deserves an award from the mayor, just like the stockbroker who saved that disgraced athlete from drowning in the East River. Lagaya deserves the keys to the city, or at least to a safe clean apartment. But she's the enemy. If her pimp stops bribing the right cops and the NYPD springs a midnight raid, she'll get arrested, imprisoned, deported.

You should hate America, Lamm tells her one Wednesday evening after they've finished. Relaxed, his pink handprints fading from her arse, he offers his advice. You should hate everything in this country, everything in this fucking city! Broadway and Forty-Second Street, the Empire State, slices of pizza the size of a steering wheel, 9/11 souvenirs three for ten bucks in Chinatown. You should hate the government, the treasury, the immigration department, the Minutemen at the border, NAFTA, the average American Joe in the average American street. Because they don't want you here. They want you in your stinking shantytown in San Salvador. You should hate American food: pretzels, French fries, burritos, sushi, chop suey, Coca-Cola in a Big Gulp cup the size of your head. This is the big generous stuff that America doesn't want to share with you. You should hate the men who raped your homeland: Reagan the Great Communicator, George the First, Don Rumsfeld, Oliver North; they armed the death squads. You should hate Americans as a species: Thomases Jefferson, Paine, Cruise and Hanks, OJ Simpson, Arnold Shwarzenegger, the cast of *Miami Vice* who taught you how to speak English. They fucked your homeland. And Australia is among the White House's closest allies, so you should hate us too. You want justice? Oliver North's a rich TV host! You *have* to hate this country. Hate the SUVs, skyscrapers, clean streets, hospitals. The finest hospitals in the world, on the same continent as your father wheezing from tuberculosis in a street flowing with shit.

You should hate me. I'm one of them.

'*I do,*' Lagaya whispered.

She was born in 1984, but the armour in her voice could have been a thousand years old.

TEN

Thursday 7 April

The night following Malik Massawi's death. Underneath the barbeque, Lamm slept, awoke, slept, awoke. Whispering at the glowing coals, on his back like a corpse in its coffin, he debated how to escape. The infuriating problem: his passport was hidden in the bottom of his sock drawer at his flat in Golders Green. And his money – the last two pay checks from the bagelry in Hendon where he worked overnight Tuesdays to Thursdays – was stashed next to the passport. His account was almost empty after paying rent; he'd planned on banking the cheques that Monday. In Lamm's wallet was £33.35, the change from the £50 note he used at the convenience store. He had a Visa card, but that was too dangerous. If the police had notified the credit card company, they'd get the call within minutes.

This headache! The vivid hurricane of a migraine enveloping Lamm's skull, brought on by the intermittent sleeplessness, the subterranean airlessness, the attempt to think a way out. He pulled up his jacket hood, trudged fifteen minutes to the convenience store at Great Cumberland Place, and bought a pack of maximum-strength aspirin and two newspapers.

Hurrying through the scrub bordering Bayswater Road, Lamm noticed three unwashed men sitting on the benches opposite Lancaster Gate. At one man's feet lay a Jack Russell terrier, filthy and asleep, looking like a taxidermist's mouldy mistake. The men gripped plastic bags, plastic cartons, plastic forks. Around midnight Wednesday through to Saturday, local vagrants gathered here to receive leftovers from a few cooks who worked in the cafés on Edgeware Road. At the padlocked gate crested by an iron griffin, the three bums patiently awaited their donated dinner of overcooked pizzas, cold fries or collapsed cheesecakes.

The homeless men weren't interested in the young fugitive. Two of them mumbled incessantly, consumed by voices of the deceased, CIA wiretaps in their skulls, telepathic orders from invisible masters. *Look at their minds*, thought Lamm, as if their skulls were glass-bottom boats. Minds mashed by alcohol, pills, mania, schizophrenia, psychosis. Mashed like tomatoes in a blender. About twenty square centimetres of their bodies, surrounding the lips and eyes, was skin-coloured; the rest a dirty overgrown lot repossessed by disorder. Madness is a careless landlord.

One of the homeless men coughed through his voluminous beard. All that biblical white hair; he resembled Moses at the shores of the Red Sea, as depicted in the watercolour by Chagall on the cover of Lamm's childhood Haggadah. Look at these unfortunate juggernauts of hair, skin, sweat! Refugees from lives unlived, swathed in their mismatched absurdity of discarded running shoes, tourists' lost hats, sweaters dropped by joggers on the walking paths. One of the vagrants wearing a frayed school blazer, another in a Tommy Hilfiger ski parka expelling foam from its seams.

After the merciless silence underground, Lamm *had* to stop here, to hear another man's voice. The muttering homeless hulks looked like they'd sat here a hundred years. Their universal uniform of chaos; these poor stinking men were the vagrants of New York too, or Rome, Moscow, Beijing, Melbourne, *anywhere*. Watery eyes, trembling porous lips, vacant stares; the incarnation of breakdown.

That's how you'll look?

They don't notice you. You're nothing to Hyde Park's derelict monarchs. Collapsed on wooden thrones, crowned by festering dreadlocks of spittle and grime, they rule their kingdom of pigeons and ghosts.

Lamm hadn't felt as sick, as unsettled, since the police helicopter last night. Not the mundane middle-class abhorrence at this homeless stink of sweat, piss, shit. No, Hyde Park's stammering wrecks so disturbed Lamm because their unremarkable disintegration was only a few rungs down from what he'd survived in New York. The living dead. Look at the flagrant fragrant hopelessness in these broken men. *There's* life's malfunction! Their nothingness is too familiar, now that you're their closest neighbour. Unlike Lewski last night, these ghosts don't disappear when you turn away. Meet your comrades in disorder: admire their yellow claws, piss-stained trousers, relentless red eyes, dead futures. *They're the actor behind your mask.*

The crinkling of a newspaper. There was a fourth man too. A grey hunchback, sitting cross-legged on the bench behind the dreadlocked hulks. Browsing through a *Daily Telegraph* fished from a garbage bin, he was Jerzy Panklowski, an arthritic bookmaker from Łódz who – way back when the mentally infirm weren't drowning beneath the tsunami of DSM diagnoses, case management reports, psycho-pharmaceutical magic bullets, mandatory institutionalization – the British would have considered a lovable eccentric.

Twenty years ago, a constable would have laughed at Jerzy's typical afternoon in Hyde Park taunting squirrels with almonds; now the police regularly bundled the hunch-backed bootmaker into a public psych ward for overnight evaluation. *The residents have complained about you.* Never once violent in his life, Jerzy was nevertheless the bogeyman to the hyper-manicured Wives of Fund Managers in town-houses opposite the park, who suspected that the hobbling old gentleman yelling insults in Polish at the pigeons was really a vicious paedophile waiting to snatch their adorable toddlers Zac and Zara Jane.

The hunchback's unintelligible mumbling suggested that, like the squirrel food, he was irreversibly nuts. The old man's life skills – his capacity to get anything done at all – falling far short of the seven habits of effectiveness as practised by Park Lane homeowners. Silver-haired in a torn oxblood suit, mouldy scarlet pullover, mud-caked loafers, Jerzy croaked hello through his ragged white beard and the smoke from half a rotten cigarette he'd found on the footpath.

'*Młody człowiek!*'

He stared at Lamm, the way he'd check a lottery ticket. The intriguing encounter – this taste of an imminent revelation? – momentarily trumped the fugitive's better judgement. Lonely, reckless Lamm! The deathly silence underground and now this crackled greeting in Polish – dulling Lamm's headache, unlocking his stiff jaw a little – induced him to sit with a crazed bootmaker who sought the same anaesthesia in conversation.

And for seventeen minutes, Lamm took in Jerzy's story with barely a breath between sentences. That the hunchback slept beneath the loading bay behind a Sainsbury's on Edgware Road, or in a Hyde Park gazebo when the weather was warm. That for sixteen years until his *katastrofa*, Jerzy was a bootmaker with his own shop on Queensway Road. Back in Łódz, he worked as a mechanic on the train lines for twenty-two years, until the wall came down and with it his contracts on the Polski Koleje Panstwowe engines thundering east to the Siberian coalfields. Spending his life savings on fake papers, Jerzy emigrated to join his older brother Janek, who tutored violin at a girls college in Shepherds Bush until his sudden death from a brain aneurysm in December 1999. Then the arthritis worsened, getting so bad that Jerzy couldn't hammer a heel without biting his tongue.

On that park bench awaiting free pizza, Max Lamm and Jerzy Panklowski sighed at the ageless phenomenon of the *annus horribilis*. Also in 1999, Jerzy's Lithuanian wife Rona – for sixteen years a seamstress in a Putney curtain factory until it relocated a hundred miles south of Beijing – returned to Vilnius to care for her ailing mother. Without his wife conscientiously regulating his medication, Jerzy ran out of his Risperidal and Zyprexa tablets. After a decade's absence, the voices returned, the paranoia resurged, and again Jerzy became convinced that the Stasi were listening to his thoughts. His angular features – the hooked nose, pinprick hazel eyes, mottled quartz skin that Heinrich Himmler condemned as subhuman in the Polish peasantry – degenerated into the hollow face that marked his four months in a Łódz schizophrenia ward during the winter of 1982.

Jerzy drank his rent money, ignored the pink eviction notices. One summer's morning he awoke in Hyde Park with his loyal friend: a one-litre mix of ginger beer and Spanish bourbon. He drank to silence the Stasi, to silence his brother's ghost playing bad notes on a broken violin, and he slept beneath the willows. That was four years ago. All this Jerzy recounted in a torrent of preformed astonishment, tinged with perverse satisfaction that he'd survived.

Jerzy crushed the empty wine cask, inhaling and clenching his fists, angry about the dungeon hell of the Łódź asylum, the estranged wife in Vilnius who had probably remarried, the bastard Moscow oligarchs who terminated his employment at the train depot, the disloyal customers who took their boots elsewhere – or wore cheap Chinese sneakers – and ruined his business. Expunging his downfall the way he'd vomit a piece of fish.

Zródlo twierdzenia!

My disaster!

Then Jerzy's twelve-minute dissertation on how you fix a pair of boots. This was Lamm's first real distraction since the Pakistani boy's skull struck the Camden pavement. You have to know the types of boot polish: naptha, turpentine, gum arabic, Kiwi Dark, Shinola, Boy Scout's, Cherry Blossom. You need a bootmaker's knowledge of scalping knives, long-nose pliers, leather shucks, flathead chisels, glued wedges, heelscrews, lacepokes, jackboots, nailguns, half-inch tacks . . .

And the bad times, the worse times, the unforgettable times in Jerzy's workshop when he heard the heavenly voice of Saint Crispin, the patron saint of bootmakers. Saint Crispin whispering in his ear canal; so clear, so *real* that Jerzy was certain it was a visitation from beyond the earthly realm. But the saint criticized Jerzy's handiwork: *your stitching is weak, the soles will split, the bootstraps will break, the toecaps will crack!* It drove the poor bootmaker to tears, to constant thoughts of suicide. Jerzy yelled at his hands, at the walls: *Kwita!* Enough! But Saint Crispin wouldn't stop the taunting. Not until the business failed.

Jerzy remembered the boots: Chelsea, cowboy, knee-high, go-go, hessian, mukluks, rigger, vlahboots, Wellingtons, giekas. You don't fix them the same way – you learn what each boot needs! *Rzeczoznawstwo!* Expertise! And the customers the bootmaker hadn't seen in five years: Tamara Kravitsky, a Russian escort who wore cherry stiletto heels that he mended three times in 1998. Elvira Eliakis, a millonaire's wife with a shoe habit to rival Imelda Marcos. Guido Guilomedes, the nightclub singer who got silver toecaps custom-moulded onto his Texan snakeskins. Eliot Katz the dentist, who every two months got his sandals steam-cleaned . . .

Lamm stared at Jerzy's eyes. Look at the spider web of wrinkles in the bootmaker's brow, etched chaotically as the memories beneath his leatherskin scalp.

'Now where are my customers? *Zdrajca!* They go to Shonofsky on Princes Square! He cannot fix a fucking heel!'

Jerzy howled, tears softening the riverbeds in his cheeks. He squeezed a final drop from the cask, then hurled it at the gate. Pop as the silvery wine-bag struck a steel spike.

The fucking Stasi broadcasting into the bootmaker's ear canal, German whispers rattling the change in his skull. Agents in the streets, snipers atop buildings, informants in the shops, buses, trains, hotels, restaurants. In Hyde Park too. *That's* why Jerzy looks at you suspiciously. You're Stasi.

The old bootmaker's reason wrung like sweat from sodden clothes. Nonetheless, he tearfully remembered customers – their faces, families, jobs, shoes – that he last encountered ten years ago.

'Now the boots come from China! The *krawiecs* don't give a fuck for workmanship!'

The bootmaker remembered another customer: Zayed Salazer, the Algerian barber in Queensway who wore sandals hand-stitched from mauve Moroccan felt.

'Zayed is a *zbrodniarz*.'

'What's that?'

'A criminal! He makes papers, passports, visas.'

The sputter of a motorcycle engine. Lamm and Jerzy spun around. Five cold pizzas were stacked at the gate.

'God bless you!' The motorcyclist wore a cook's white smock.

'*Podziekowanie!* Bless you!'

Jerzy hobbled over to the pizzas. Lamm remained on the park bench.

Tomorrow, you must visit Zayed the barber.

ELEVEN

Friday 8 April

Lamm's uneasy sleep. The dream playing like a looped video tape: Malik Massawi dead on the pavement, then rising like a zombie until the bottle smashed into his skull and he died another death. For a few awful seconds, he lay still until he stood up. Then the fatal blow, he fell dead, and again stood up, got hit, fell down, got up and so on. Three hours of the jack-in-a-box nightmare, or three minutes? When Lamm awoke, basted in sweat, he remembered every bloody detail.

10.37 a.m.

Time for your excursion.

On the way, Lamm stopped at an underground public toilet. He shaved, brushed his teeth, dispensed liquid soap upon his palms and rubbed the lather onto his underarms, forearms, face, neck. He washed his T-shirt and shirt in the basin, wrung them dry beneath a hand-dryer. You must make a good impression.

Wearing his jacket hood, blending among the tourists, shoppers, pedestrians, Lamm emerged from Kensington Gardens at the blunt top of Queensway Road. This shopping strip incorporating the Tube station, the beige sandstone Hilton and a subterranean bowling alley where, four nights a week, teenage gangs congregate outside to swap stolen phones, compare their elephantine jeans and steal each other's fake gold chains. On the same block: a Western Union booth where janitors and taxi drivers send money home to East Africa; tourist shops selling Princess Di aprons and Union Jack coffee mugs made in Taiwan; two discount supermarkets for the backpackers, five souvlaki bars, and three velvety Persian lounges where Egyptian men recline on tasselled cushions, watch Al Jazeera and smoke hookahs like the gigantic slug in *Alice in Wonderland*.

Lamm entered Queensway Arcade. A miniature shopping mall with creaky plywood floors, housing Ukrainian leather merchants hawking the fashions of 1981; a tobacconist selling the usual assortment of bongs, flick-knives and Bob Marley T-shirts; two foreign-language DVD stalls (one Russian, one Arabic) trading pirated discs; a plasterboard internet café crowded with Australian backpackers updating their résumés; a coffee lounge frequented by local businessmen wearing unbuttoned silk shirts, spitting specks of hummus upon their furry chests as they argued in Farsi about the war, the bastards at the immigration department, or the crazy hook-handed preacher spruiking Bin Laden's vitriol at the Finsbury Park mosque.

Deep in the arcade opposite a tarot stall, a tiny barber shop rattled to Egyptian pop music. Here was Zayed Salazar; a tall, bald Algerian wearing a lilac shirt and the Moroccan felt sandals that so fascinated Jerzy the bootmaker. No customers; the barber attended to a fax machine spitting out an official-looking document. He turned as the masonite floor creaked beneath Lamm's sneakers.

'My second customer today! How much you want off?' Zayed glanced at Lamm's hair. His smile faded.

'The shampoo cost you extra.'

'I'm not here for a haircut.'

The barber's eyes narrowed to slits.

'Come into my office.'

Lamm stood in a warm little room crammed with a laptop, fax machine, colour laser printer and scanner on the desk, unopened boxes of shampoo on the floor, a digital camera on a tripod. With slender bony hands, the barber frisked Lamm from his collar to his ankles.

'Who told you about me?'

The barber glared into Lamm's bloodshot eyes. Does he see your sleeplessness, your guilt, your nightmare?

'Jerzy. The Polish bootmaker.'

Zayed's eyebrows shot skywards. He laughed.

'Jerzy! The old Polish nut! Where is he? I heard he's living on the street?'

'He's not well:

'Not well? I *loved* that man. Tell him to see me, give him my number. Tell him my sandals need fixing.'

The barber scrawled his mobile phone number onto a card specked with a customer's hair, then slid it into Lamm's shirt pocket.

'I don't ask questions. Payment must be in advance. An EU passport is £5,000. An American is eight, they're harder to get. I also do Pakistan and India. It takes two months, usually longer. You won't find a better price in London, but if you do, I will go five per cent cheaper and give you three months' free haircuts. Understand?'

Lamm nodded. The impossibility – the dangerous futility of it all! – churning his gut.

Eight thousand pounds.

He knows you're broke. It's written on your face.

'If you don't want a haircut, goodbye. Call me if you get the money.'

TWELVE

Eight thousand pounds. What the home entertainment system in Kelly Wesson's penthouse cost her father. His presidential ambition everywhere in that Park Lane apartment, the Minotaur's home away from home when he visited Europe to speak at Tory fundraisers, attend NATO talk fests or shout scarlet-faced tirades at the naïve peaceniks from the International Atomic Energy Agency. Antique oak sideboards, walnut floorboards, burgundy velvet drapes, by the front door a US flag (a restored relic from an Iwo Jima gunboat), in the master bedroom a four-poster bed carved during the Civil War (of the same vintage as the bed in the White House's Lincoln Bedroom) where the senator's daughter got to work on her intriguing new boy from the barbeque. Only the best here: a gleaming Miele kitchen that Kelly never used; a £2 million view of Hyde Park, but she preferred the curtains drawn. The shelves lined with unread first editions inscribed with the author's best wishes to the senator. Fat autographed books by Dr Kissinger, Samuel Huntingdon, Norm Podhoretz, Margaret Thatcher, Tom Clancy . . .

In the master bedroom, Lamm was fascinated by the mantelpiece. A procession of framed photographs showing the Minotaur shaking hands with Gorbachev, Putin,

Mitterand, Chirac; with the Chinese premier surrounded by henchmen in penguin suits, with Yitzhak Rabin and every Israeli PM since, and with every US president back to Nixon except for Clinton. Were these photographs, Lamm wondered, what Wesson's wife Janet LaRoye, manicured K Street lobbyist and potential first lady, gazed at when the Minotaur bent her over and fucked her the way he fucked the Chinese over steel tariffs? Did the photo of the senator hunting with Dick Cheney help Mrs Wesson to come, whilst her husband groaned like a walrus during a pastime almost as satisfying to him as shooting doves with the vice-president?

Or were the photos on the mantelpiece the *senator's* turn-on, so he climaxed upon looking at himself and Newt Gingrich meeting the crazy dictator of North Korea in his Mao-suit? What Senator Wesson did in his London penthouse to his wife, he'd do to the communist madmen in Pyongyang. Fuck them up the arse. So hard that the sneaky bastards can't sit at the nuclear negotiating table. Fuck them mercilessly, so they know who's really the boss in East Asia!

This occurred to Lamm during his first bewildering tryst with Kelly, who was surprisingly resistant down there despite her ravenous appetites. Eyes shut, she arched her fake-tanned legs around his shoulders. 'More,' she breathed. That grenade of a word stimulating the sex-crazy homunculus in a man's mind that's resistant to rationality, common sense or cynicism. Lamm obeyed the request, moaning incoherently as his lips clasped the sweet hollow of her neck.

They met that Friday afternoon. Lamm hunched in the uncut grass by the barbeque, eating cold pumpkin pie, listening to the Radio 4 news on his pocket radio while he examined the *Guardian*, the *Sun* and the *Evening Standard* for news of the manhunt. Probably Hyde Park's most secluded grove; the tourists kept to the grand leafy avenues, the joggers to the tracks. So when he heard twigs crushing behind him, Lamm jolted upright. The adrenaline surge: dilated nostrils, sudden sweat, a tight chest.

Something poked the bare skin above Lamm's belt. A soft wet nudge that was, in the half-second before he spun around, not unpleasant.

A white Scottish terrier. The dog's bottomless black eyes looked up, requesting a pat, a snack, a walk. The terrier licked Lamm's outstretched arm.

'Hello, doggie.'

The dog whimpered, shuffling into Lamm's lap. Look at the collar: CASPAR. After two days alone in stale grease, there was resurrective pleasure in scratching a little dog's hairy ears.

'*Caspar! Casp-aaar! Caspar!*'

A girl shouting. An American girl, perhaps five minutes' walk away. Her voice taut with the finest pedigree of Northeastern pronunciation. A Kennedy-esque dialect as exclusively reared as this snow-white terrier.

'*Caspar!*'

The dog jumped, barking. But Lamm grabbed its collar. Insanely, recklessly, but there was something – so much! – intriguing about the girl's voice. Her sugary babyish affectation, the anglified clipped vowels characteristic of Andover or Phillips Exeter or some other prep school, nevertheless tinged with desperation. Her enunciation of anxiety; of a powerlessness temporarily akin to Lamm's own. Anxious, overwhelmed because her pampered little dog had chased a squirrel into the shrubs.

'*Casp-aaar! Caspar!*'

Listen to the shaky timbre in her voice; she'd do anything to get Caspar back. *Anything.* Crafty, conniving Lamm! His second brain hardened as the girl called for her beloved.

The terrier barked, Lamm gripped its collar. You're properly excited now, and why not? It's the voice of a classy, vulnerable girl, up against the odds. Pandora ignoring her better judgement. Don't let the dog go. Keep barking, Caspar, and reel her in! The girl's voice reminded Lamm of two women especially: Barbara Walters, the hypermanicured anchorwoman embalmed like Lenin although she's alive and well, and a talented porno star named Haley Wilde whom he once watched on DVD at a buck's night and later mentally resurrected while he took a hot spa.

Through the flowerbeds, bushes, trees, Kelly Wesson followed the barking to its source.

'Caspar! I was worried about you!"

She grabbed the dog. No hesitation shoving her fingers into the lap of a dirt-streaked stranger.

'You arsehole! You were holding him from me!"

Up to Lamm's eye level, she wore vintage cowboy boots – pilfered from her father's collection – and navy riding pants that could have easily cost £1,000 at a Saville Row tailor appointed to Her Majesty. A grey T-shirt masterfully hugged Kelly's slim midriff and the small hard precipice of her breasts. Nothing printed on the T-shirt, but the way it fit suggested that its price tag wasn't far behind the riding pants. Her hair tied up at the back, strawberry-gold wisps blurry in the fading sunlight. Lips glossy despite the wind. And her neck! A graceful marvel of physiology, surely containing twice as many vertebrae as the average girl's. Sweat glistened off Kelly's bare skin; the innumerable watery diamonds that already Lamm wanted to lick off, to taste her salt. No eye shadow nor eyeliner, though her eyebrows were expertly shaped; not a rebellious stray hair on her face to betray that undiluted femininity.

And her eyes! Immense yet fragile vitality in there, burning amid the world-weariness of having learnt things the hard way. The hard, insensible, destructive way; Lamm recognized that look. Most captivating in Kelly's stare: insatiability, adventurousness, recklessness. Her eyes promising, before another word was said, that she wasn't the usual Park Lane princess who'd run home to cry about the nasty bum who stole her doggie. Sure, she resembled a Boston Brahmin pampered ever since she swallowed the silver spoon. But, Lamm sensed, this girl was no stranger to transgression. He stared into her pale blue eyes, definitely for too long, and she didn't flinch a bit.

'Your dog wanted to run away from you. I kept him here.'

She cocked a sliver of an eyebrow.

'I bet. And why would my Caspar want to run away from *me*?'

'Ask him.'

She's staring at you. *Really* staring. Your face, hands, body. Doesn't believe a word of your shit. Can she tell that you're nuts? That you were an athlete before you became a vagrant? That you're a murderer? A Jew?

Lamm folded the *Guardian* shut. On the front page was Malik Masawi's funeral. He flipped the paper upside down.

'Take a seat. We're both foreigners in a foreign land.'

'I prefer to stand.'

The terrier purred like a cat while she scratched its ears. Never seen that before.

'So why is a girl like you talking to someone like me? You got your teddy bear back.'

Kelly rubbed the dog's neck. Her tight brow softening, tension draining from her face. That dog's like the Chinese relaxation balls you grind in the palm of your hand.

Or *you're* her relaxation?

'Let's say that I suffer from an insatiable addiction to ruining my life, and the lives of those around me. Sound familiar?'

She didn't look away from his eyes. Didn't flinch. Curious, emboldened.

'So Mr Crocodile Hunter, why are you sleeping in the park? Already shot this week's rent money up your arm?'

'I'm having a picnic.'

'Some picnic.'

She glanced at Lamm's lunch. 'You sleep under the barbeque, don't you?'

Tell her to go away. It's safer that way.

Look at the new permutation in her formerly sarcastic features. Fascination. Is it pity prompting this princess to engage with a bum like you? Or the prospect of a new game? You're today's diversion from her emptiness. From the truth. The hunger for what she shouldn't have.

Was it so easy for the Sirens to lure sailors to their deaths?

'Aren't you gonna ask me for a shower and a hot meal? My name's Kelly. Today I'm your good Samaritan.'

He expected her to ask his name. Instead, she untangled Caspar's leash, then walked through the overgrown path.

Ha! Only a fool, a sex freak or a madman would follow her!

They approached the apartment building; she hadn't spoken another word. Hadn't asked Lamm why, on a sunny day, he was wearing a hood. Probably guessed.

Walking up the steps, Lamm nearly fell backwards. His father was floating by the door.

Lamm's father's ghost – the living have ghosts too? – wore a blue tennis shirt, white shorts and sneakers. His face salmon-pink, moustache quivering furiously, right arm brandishing a racquet like a policeman's truncheon.

'Max, I *cannot* believe this! Would Krickstein throw his life down the drain for a *shtup*? Look what happened to Boris Becker when he got a blowjob in the closet of a Japanese restaurant! And *you*! You've only got your life to lose!'

But Lamm's father always talked too much. As the parental tirade reverberated in Lamm's ear canal, he'd already entered the gilded lobby. Too late, and not a policeman in sight.

Kelly hit the polished walnut button for the top floor.

'Get in. Take your shoes off at the door.'

THIRTEEN

'Don't come yet,' she breathed. Lamm marvelled at how Kelly's incendiary moans lured him against his better judgement. *But many smarter, greater men than you have risked everything for a clandestine fuck. Profumo. Mitterand. JFK. Clinton.* As usual during the business end of their business, Lamm stared at the mantelpiece. At the photograph of Senator Wesson and Newt Gingrich shaking hands with the crazy North Korean dictator. It helped to postpone Lamm's climax, seeing those wrinkled carpetbaggers greeting the Dear Leader on a flowery podium in Pyongyang.

Everything in the apartment was chrome, gold or wrapped in an endangered skin. The whole place – twice featured in the UK edition of *Vogue Living* – had been decorated (at £100 an hour) by an interior designer described by Kelly's father as 'the queer who did Princess Di's restrooms'. Typical décor for one of the US Senate's wealthiest representatives, no less extravagant in his London getaway where occasionally he entertained Westminster's cabinet ministers. Kelly's father was her rock, her ball and chain, her blank cheque. Silver-haired with a horse's shaggy eyebrows, small blue eyes, capped teeth and a pink trunk for a neck, Senator Wesson was an orator renowned for soapbox tirades that reminded historically astute listeners of the Nuremburg rallies, or George Wallace assailing the desegregationist protesters at the University of Alabama, or both. For eleven years, ever since a *Washington Post* cartoonist caricatured him as an enraged bull wearing a pinstriped suit, Senator Wesson had been dubbed 'The Minotaur' by his eternal enemies – the lefty editors at the *New York Times*, the lefty essayists at the *New York Review of Books*, and the lefty yid hacks every Sunday on *Meet the Press*. And the nickname stuck.

Amongst his many enemies, the Minotaur was truly hated. Hated with vehemence exceptional even for the gutters and pork barrels of Capitol Hill. Disliked for his neoconservative allegiances (dating back to his Skull & Bones days at Yale), for his apocalyptic fear mongering about Saddam's WMDs all through 2002, for his tireless efforts at destroying the Clintons from Gennifer Flowers through to Paula Jones through to Whitewater through to Monica's cumstained cocktail dress.

Of course, he never gave a shit about the tree-hugging, bagel-fucking, chardonnay-quaffing, jihad-sympathising unAmericans forever sneering down from their solar powered rats' nests up on the Upper East Side or the Hollywood hills. A deputy Secretary of Defence from '88 to '92 under George the First, worth $150 million from golden handshakes and Pentagon oil contracts, a long-time mentor to Oliver North, hunting partner to the vice-president and Jim Baker, patron of the American Enterprise Institute, for decades a favourite houseguest at Ron and Nancy's Californian ranch, Senator Richard Wesson was the man most likely to eulogize Dr Kissinger when that leather-skinned warhorse goes to the great US Embassy in the sky. And if he could convince a sceptical Washington press corps that he wasn't out to repeal *Roe v Wade* and unilaterally nuke the Iranians, if the Republican National Committee might just ignore his draft-dodging in 1968, the messy $10 million divorce from his first wife and a 1985 conviction for drunk driving, then one day, it was suggested by those in the know, the Minotaur would get a shot at the Oval Office.

In return for her allowance of a thousand dollars a week – most of it spent on cocaine, an unremarkable indulgence among the rich bored children of Washington's elite – Kelly played her vital, phony role. Her first and only job, pretending to be the Minotaur's happy, perfect, patriotic twenty-year-old daughter at Capitol Hill galas and GOP fundraisers. She'd met three Mr Presidents, dined four times in the Long Room of the White House, attended movie premieres at the handwritten invitation of Mel Gibson or Charlton Heston, played mixed doubles on the grass court at Dick Cheney's holiday ranch, even landed in a Chinook on an aircraft carrier for a photo-op with Daddy. And she hated every minute of it.

Kelly was bored by her polite familiarity with America's – the world's – most powerful men and she could predict, to a word, the patronising comments these upstanding grey fat cats invariably uttered to her. Her father's dinner guests – the four-star generals, Fortune 500 CEOs and campaign donors of outstanding generosity – loved meeting Kelly, loved mentally undressing her firm amber body, loved flirting with her, and she fuelled Lolitaesque fantasies for these sixtysomething Roger Ramjets during the final futile sorties of their virility. Perhaps one day she'd fuck one of the rich decorated sleazebags, just to irk Daddy. Some of the generals still had taut stomachs and the features of John Wayne. She liked to imagine these humourless, All-American military types whimpering like kittens as they ejaculated, their stony faces suited to Mount Rushmore, not to licking a twenty-year-old heiress' pussy. It'd be kinky, and even more fun if she snorted a little blow beforehand.

But despite the invitations to parties gatecrashed by paparazzi, a Z-series BMW soft-top for Christmas and her genetic jackpot of the hourglass figure, stratospheric cheekbones and golden hair routinely endowed by wealthy parentage, Kelly Wesson wanted to kill herself. Her life wasn't uniformly unpleasurable – she loved cocaine (and hash, speed, meth, OxyContin, Seroquel or Valium) that she got from the drug-dealing son of a Virginian congressman – but ultimately these syrups, pills, rocks and powders deepened her despair. Kelly habituated to the narcotics, needing more, then more, to quell the terrors, to fog over her irrefutable desire not to exist. To stop her from doing *it*. And if half a day passed without a hit, on came the withdrawal symptoms. Trembling hands, dizziness, cold sweats, the nausea erupting whatever morsel she last ate, the sickening sensation of ten thousand pin-legged insects colonising her skin; all getting worse, unbearably, until finally she snorted a line and exhaled the panic skywards.

Barely old enough to buy a beer, Kelly Wesson was drowning in a medicated abyss at any time, all the time. Drowning down, down, down into her daily misery of mollycoddled boredom, of unyielding insomnia, of mood swings, migraines, bulimia, anorexia, anaemia, of waking alone at three every afternoon in that silent Georgetown mansion with spookily high ceilings where nobody ever told her *not* to kill herself. A dull crushing existence dictated by her dealers, by a conniving bitch of a stepmother and a famous statue of a father, by the inescapable attention bestowed by her surname, by the poisonous anaesthesia facilitated by the money. The unendurable facts of Kelly Wesson's glamorous, perfect life.

It got worse. Eighteen months into her descent, Kelly wouldn't – couldn't – crawl out of bed at 4 p.m. without shooting a speedball to forget who she was and wasn't. February 2004, the end approached. All day, she envisaged the obvious solutions: go hang yourself from the dining-room chandelier. Gas yourself in the Hummer that nobody ever drives. Gulp four packets of Valiums like they're Tic-Tacs. Blow your brains out with the .45 that Daddy keeps under his bed. Hurl an empty backpack at the president's motorcade and get shot by the Secret Service, or, best of all, jump off the Washington Monument to forever disgrace *him*. The deadly intentions only delayed by what she smoked in foil, popped down her throat, shot into her arm, snorted up her nose.

She awoke around 5.30 a.m. most mornings, after three hours' sleep. Her throat taut, fingers trembling, forehead beaded in cold sweat. Using her stepmother's silver nail scissors, Kelly sometimes cut her palms. The precise slash: your bloody flagellation for waking up too early. She cut herself for eating too much, for crying too much, for being stupid, for being fat, for being a coward, for being alone. She cut herself for cutting herself. For being alive. *So fucking do it!* But you can't. A failure at suicide too, although she told nobody. Months earlier, Kelly had thrown her mobile into the goldfish pond because, when her bulimia hit Georgetown's gossip circles, some cheerleading friends started calling up with their questions. Their dumb fucking questions, asked in the soft, 'sensitive' whine perfected by Oprah, Tyra, Barbara Walters, Katie Couric. *Would you like to get a coffee and talk? . . . You need to give yourself a holiday from you! . . . I feel what you're going through . . . I understand your pain! . . .* these fucking anorexia survivors with a Mother Teresa complex. They wouldn't stop calling, so Kelly drowned the phone.

Despite a pantry downstairs the size of a tool shed, stocked with the best food from the Beltway's best delis, Kelly ate only jelly babies, seaweed crackers and Weight Watchers microwave pizza. Anything else she regurgitated, gaining unparalleled knowledge of Washington's most exclusive toilet bowls. No matter how far into the afternoon she slept, or how much instant coffee she slurped for breakfast at 5 p.m., Kelly felt insurmountably weak until she got high, and soon she weighed not much more than Dwight, her father's Great Dane guarding the front gate.

Those six months in 2003 – The Terror, with her father away on business as Operation Iraqi Freedom drew nearer – Kelly lay on her bed every afternoon, all afternoon, debating the only question that mattered. '*Today!*', she sobbed into her pillow, trying to convince herself that *now*, not tonight after she fed the dog, not tomorrow after she farewelled the chauffer, not the next day, but *now*, this torturous fucking instant, was the moment to be brave, to be strong or unremittingly stupid, and to finally, unhesitatingly kill herself. But owing to her fear of pain, or the cruel stubborn joke that was her desire to live, Kelly couldn't do it.

Most days, she stole her father's gun from underneath his bed, loaded a round, clicked it shut, then collapsed into his Chesterfield recliner. Waiting. Trying. Yearning. But no matter Kelly's anticipation for the-relief-in-not-being, no matter the stark unendurable featurelessness of everything in her life apart from death, she couldn't peer down the barrel and thoughtlessly pull the trigger. *You dumb fat coward bitch!* She'd lay twenty Valiums next to a glass of water, look at them for three hours, at every millimetre-long fissure in their bleak powdered forms, but she couldn't gulp them unthinkingly the way Dwight wolfed down his dog biscuits. Kelly remembered war memorials that she had visited for official functions; the nameless millions who perished in the World Wars, Korea and Vietnam. Angrily, she foresaw the monstrous death toll from her father's new Iraqi adventure. What difference is one more death? But it is *your* death, so pulling the trigger is no easy thing. Kelly hated life, but was afraid not to live and couldn't understand why. You love to hate. That's what you love? The hatred.

This wasn't the usual adolescent phase of hysterics and histrionics, of life lessons learnt riding the teenage girl's merry-go-round of broken hearts and hollow tears. Much too real for that. Long ago, Kelly dismissed as a fairytale that her descent would end in anything apart from a funeral. But still, she couldn't swallow Daddy's gun and pull her index finger an inch! Couldn't force herself.

Do it.

Now!

But then, that would be it. Irreversible. What they don't show on teen melodramas: the one-way death. You're a stupid fat coward, always were. Indecisive too; the more to decide, the more you can't. Even at dying, you're a screw-up. Another reason to kill yourself.

But you can't.

So always – although for nearly a hundred afternoons that

year, Kelly sat in her father's recliner staring down the barrel, at her trigger finger, tearful yet drained of tears, occasionally motionless as she revisited what fancifully seemed like a happy childhood back in Dallas ten years ago – when the senator returned home, his gun was back in its usual place. In a briefcase underneath his bed, in case an Al-Qaeda assassin ever breached the guards and CCTV cameras outside. Kelly hid the noose she tied from a handmade skipping rope that her mother had sent from Paris as a birthday present; she stockpiled her sleeping pills in the billiards room inside an antique globe of the world, and she waited for her day of courage, of abandon, of deathly liberation to miraculously approach. Kelly's father and stepmother knew nothing of her desperate intentions; they were busy with their schedule of media launches, confirmation hearings, campaign fundraisers, gala banquets, press briefings, weekend trips on the Learjet, grouse hunts down in Texas, shouting matches against Christopher Hitchens or James Carville on *Larry King Live*, and so forth.

Nobody except Kelly's dealers knew the extent of her addictions, for skilfully she concealed her stonewashed skin, sudden nosebleeds, pockmarked arms and vertiginous mood swings. On Thursday afternoons, she visited an 'organic' beauty salon at the upscale end of North Street, Georgetown, opposite the handsome townhouse at number 3307 where Jack Kennedy hosted a cocktail party the afternoon of his inauguration. At $175 a session, the beauticians did a fake tan, a facial using mud from a magical geyser in Ecuador, a whole body defoliation, a herbal shampoo and, owing to Kelly's distinguished parentage, threw in a Brazilian wax for free. Though she barely slept nor ate, Kelly nevertheless resembled one of the flawless Aryan cherubs from Leni

Riefenstahl's pageant films glorifying the Nazi Olympics of 1936.

Inevitably, she was pursued by dozens of eligible Beltway bachelors, fresh from Yale or Stanford law school. The onslaught of dinner invitations increased following Kelly's appearance wearing a low-cut Lacroix gown, statuesquely gaunt, guzzling Bollinger at her father's sixtieth birthday bash alongside Arnold Schwarzenegger and the president's blonde nieces in a *Vanity Fair* puff-piece entitled 'Versailles on the Potomac'. But Kelly hated her admirers, these arrogant young lawyers, congressional interns and K Street lobbyists for whom she was merely a trophy fuck and a stepping-stone into Daddy's inner circle. So the day in late 2003 when she mysteriously passed her truant final year at the Georgetown prep school that enjoyed her family's patronage, Kelly decided to do what she really wanted. She'd get far, far away from Washington DC, from the silent mansion hastening her suicide. Far away from Senator Richard Davis Wesson and all that his prominence inflicted upon her.

But first, the Minotaur's Faustian pact: you must serve nine months at the National Guard of Maryland. The senator – who never showed interest in his daughter's aspirations when they shared the limo on route to a banquet – was nevertheless incensed that, unlike her older brother Tommy the hotshot attorney, Kelly refused to sit the entrance exam for a prep school in Connecticut that specialized in getting troublemakers like her into Yale.

Kelly couldn't cram a year's algebra and chemistry into three months! She barely stayed awake without cigarettes and speed. Senator Wesson was in many ways a neglectful father – or a deadbeat dad, as he'd once publicly dubbed a black auto worker from Detroit who took paid leave so he could join the Million Man March – but he recognized that, above anything else, what Kelly required was discipline. *Discipline*: that indispensable quality of the military that, the senator liked to say, had won the United States the Cold War and every war since. The Minotaur was legendarily stubborn – he once endured a nine-hour filibuster against a gun control bill without leaving for a toilet break – and he made up his mind. The National Guard would put Kelly on the right track.

He made the offer she couldn't refuse. If Kelly agreed to nine months of service in the National Guard, he would facilitate her ideal escape. She'd relocate to London, all expenses paid, to study at an exclusive art college that she'd read about in *Vogue*. The Central Saint Martins College of Art and Design on Charing Cross Road. The *alma mater* for many eminent fashion designers – Galliano, McQueen, McCartney, et al – Saint Martins would, Kelly presumed, be a fun, respectable escape from hell at home on the Capitol catwalk. Despite the scarred forearms and dark bags beneath her eyes (concealed by make-up), despite the scorched teaspoons and foil pipes amassed in her lingerie drawer, Kelly nevertheless recognized the value of a quality education; its absence was etched into the hollow crevassed faces of teenage crack addicts, those emaciated black or Hispanic kids with huge eyes, who begged her for change on the bus she rode uptown to Columbia Heights for a twenty-dollar-bag of rocks when her regular dealer, the Virginian congressman's son, was away in Vail at the family ski lodge. On her rare, painless afternoons when the sun was out and she wasn't compelled to steal Daddy's gun from underneath his bed, Kelly liked to sunbake in the gazebo and browse her stepmother's magazines. *Vogue, Marie Claire, Cosmopolitan, Harper's Bazaar.* Those fat glossies smelling like the beauty counter at Macy's. Must-have clothes draped upon catwalk models who, though taller and even skinnier than Kelly, wore her own expression of unassailable drug-addled haughtiness. One day in April, she read an article in *Vogue* about London's most exclusive fashion college. Ten seconds later, she made up her mind.

Kelly typed 'saint martins london' into Google. There it was: the Undergraduate Diploma in Fashion and Communications . . . and she *could* dress, she could talk . . . could the diploma be much harder than that? An ideal escape, this London art college full of kids as wealthy and illicitly medicated as she, where the name Richard Wesson, she was certain, meant nothing. Better yet, an ocean would separate Kelly from her father and stepmother. Kelly accurately foresaw that Saint Martins offered a smorgasbord of stylish, opinionless boys who, instead of balking at transgression like her geeky Georgetown classmates hell-bent on med school or the State Department, unashamedly thirsted for drugs, fucking and more drugs. Her three favourite things. Anticipating her anonymous unchaperoned new life, a smile came to Kelly's lips; an inartificial smile, unrelated to the mundane opiate rush, that was in itself a rare event. What the Minotaur demanded, he would get. Even the military. Because Kelly *had* to go to London.

'It's hard work, but it's worth every minute,' the senator proclaimed on the eve of Kelly's departure, on the phone from a G8 summit in the French Alps. 'The military will stop your vapid, indulgent lifestyle. It'll stop your days of waking up at 3 p.m. instead of using your talents, whatever they are. When I was your age I had a helluva time in the Texas Air Guard, I went there instead of Saigon.' He paused in vain for her affirmation. 'Stay the nine months. Make me proud. Make *your country* proud. Then take the first plane to London and I guarantee, you'll get the apartment.'

Kelly hadn't another way out. Reject her father's offer and she was forbidden from moving anywhere, owing to mysterious 'security risks'. Whenever she was prohibited from anything – a solo trip to Miami to see her uncle Robert's new golf resort, or a fortnight in LA way back when she didn't need a snort of speed merely to leave the house – her father invoked the spectre of 'security risks'. There are, he would say, *unsavoury individuals* out there. *People who wish to do you harm.* Evildoers. Terrorists. Although the senator wouldn't specify who these unsavoury people actually were.

'To know the specifics wouldn't be in your best interest.'

'Dad! I want the facts! Or do I have to read them in the *New York Times*? Who's this week's ZZ Top lookalike in a cave in Pakistan? It's not fair! You don't let me know *anything*!'

But the man who famously stonewalled Congress over Oliver North's indictment wouldn't capitulate to his bratty daughter at the dinner table. She wanted information that was classified. Off-limits. It never swayed the Minotaur that in his presence, Kelly cunningly took his side. She'd curse his usual enemies: Graydon Carter and the liberal lapdogs at *Vanity Fair*, the vengeful Clintonites plotting their revenge, the investigative reporters up in New York – those fucking Hershes and Finkleblooms at the *New Yorker* – endlessly digging dirt on the Minotaur's share dealings for another five-thousand-word hatchet piece. Expertly she regurgitated her father's tirades, mimicked his prejudices, kindled his longstanding vendettas, not because she gave a shit but to get what *she* wanted out of him – a bigger allowance; a labradoodle puppy; an exemption from summer camp, or, most recently, the truth about whether a terrorist threat against her life did, in fact, exist.

Feeling a rare tingle of pride in his daughter, the senator recognized his own deviousness in Kelly. But he wouldn't budge, never divulging a thing she couldn't learn from the *Washington Post* that she never read. Sometimes extra guards patrolled the mansion's perimeter, or another surveillance camera was installed atop the ivy-encrusted fence, but Kelly wasn't allowed to know why. Had a terrorist suspect confessed, during his waterboarding in an Egyptian torture chamber, that Senator Wesson's family was a target? Had a suspicious package arrived in the mail, like the anthrax letters that stalked the capital three years earlier? Kelly knew that she didn't know anything, and it drove her nuts.

Only at home, drinking with his few trusted pals, did Kelly glimpse her father at rest. When the tight pink knot of his brow unravelled, the hangman's glare softened, and for an hour or two, he seemed at peace. Away from TV cameras, journalists and women, amidst the foul-mouthed camaraderie that, it seemed, he cherished more than his daughter. Kelly was struck by the liberated physicality of the senator and his buddies drinking out on the porch; catching up, reminiscing, talking politics, telling dirty jokes, laughing with tears in their hard blue eyes, hugging, patting, touching; these immaculately groomed brutes in unbuttoned Western shirts and cowboy boots, often loud and rancorous, yet intermittently surveying each other with long, quiet, gritty stares, each man's eyes fixed at the other's moist lips, that conveyed more in their silence than she imagined.

The first Saturday of every month, the Minotaur and the handful of Washington men that he liked – usually his campaign director Garett Dunlap, the powerful attorney Larry Gibson (a partner to the distinguished old lawyer that Dick Cheney mistook for a grouse and shot) and Paul Leniston the deputy Treasury secretary, all three of them divorced – sat together on the back porch eating cheesesteaks, drinking Belgian beers, smoking cigars and howling like a pack of marmosets. They talked foreign policy, outdoing each other at thinking up names for that week's newsworthy villain. *Those Cairo camelfuckers . . . Baathist French frogs . . . arse-nosed AIPACsteins . . . Baghdad beard bombers . . . Missile-munching martyrs . . . Caracas commie crackpots . . . Pyongyang pyjama poobahs . . . Saddamite sodomites . . .* on they'd go until three in the morning. Georgetown mansion or not, what the Minotaur loved was a grimy Texas saloon and inside its drunken banter and sweaty oily chests unbuttoned at the bar after a long day's hauling machinery. A place like Howie's, the sports bar in South Dallas where he'd cut his first oil deals, where Captain Hazelwood, the guy who crashed the *Exxon Valdez* up in Alaska, drank away his legal troubles for a while. The timeless truckstop havens of simple pungent smells: fossilized peanuts, sticky carpet, vomit in the washbasin, dried semen on the toilet seat, stale sweat. Wesson first loved those dank bars in his youth as an amateur boxing promoter. In 1969, the *Kansas Midwestern Star* tipped him to become 'the white Don King', but owing to his father's connections, he went to Yale instead.

Relaxing on the mansion's porch with a bottle of good Scotch, they let it all out.

'Dick, you're wrong about the pussies making a fuss in the *Post*,' Larry Gibson slurred on a warm evening in September 2003. 'It doesn't matter what brand of bullshit the spooks cooked up. We could nuke Saddam back to the Stone Age and the kids today, they *will* accept it. This ain't Chicago in 1968, this ain't Berkeley back when we were terrified of the draft. Nowadays, the college students don't wanna get arrested barricading Penn Avenue. They want good grades. They want a PlayStation. They want a Honda. They wanna get laid. My nephew Paul's no dummy, he's at med school at Tufts, and he wouldn't know his Sunni from his Shi'ite from his sunny shit.' Gibson guffawed into his glass; the tipsy habit of laughing at your own wisecracks.

'How about your kid?' Leniston asked Wesson. 'The blonde bombshell. Marilyn. She ever turn your dinner table into *Meet the Press*?'

The Minotaur laughed, the rumble of a grizzly feasting on a hiker. 'My daughter doesn't disapprove of what I stand for. Not that I'm aware of.'

Wesson sat up, facing the patio door.

'Be honest, my dear. What do you *really* think of us? Are we a quartet of wrinkled, warmongering old beasts?'

The other men cracked up like schoolboys. 'Dick, give the girl a break! How about another drink?'

Kelly crept away from the door. *How did he know you were listening?* Drunk or not, the Minotaur rarely missed a thing.

Later that night on the mansion porch, Wesson told stories of the decrepit Midwestern boxing halls – in Kansas City, Topeka, Des Moines, Jackson – where, by manipulating his saps in the ring and the drunken suckers in the betting circle, he first learnt the how-to of politics. How to control desperate people via their deficiencies. Eighteen-year-old Dick Wesson, a ginger-haired rake just graduated from Fort Worth Methodist High in 1967, taking bets while his bone-headed cowpokes got ready on the ropes. He never forgot those farmyard fighters; the way they trusted him unreservedly, their blunt resilience, their bleeding gums, their ripped pummelled abdomens trailing silvery lines of perspiration down into their tight full undershorts. He'd pick them up at rough bars after the harvest, so broke they'd use a cut of orange peel for a mouthguard. His right hand deep in his pocket, gleefully fondling $500 and something else too, Dick Wesson watched his pairs of bare-chested Tom Joads duke it out for peanuts while the rural crowds went berserk. Everything that, thirty-five years later, had taken him into the loftiest federal offices and boardrooms in America, Senator Richard Wesson first learnt in a dusty Oklahoma City boxing hall where both fighters turned out to be the loser.

FOURTEEN

March 2004

Kelly agreed to join the National Guard. So the Minotaur made the phone call. On his mobile phone, during lunchbreak the afternoon that the 9/11 Commission heard Richard Clarke's told-you-so testimony that uncannily reminded Wesson of his ex-wife's gin-soaked tirades. Down the line at the Maryland barracks, the lieutenant was perfectly cooperative. After six weeks' training, the senator's daughter would get an officer's post.

At Union station, Kelly got a farewell hug from Ray, her octogenarian chauffer and the only black man since emancipation to visit her family's cotton ranch near Charleston. She rode the train, not an airplane, because hidden in her toiletries bag were five ounces of pot, a miniature hash pipe and $2,000 worth of cocaine, shrink-wrapped inside tampons and a jumbo bottle of moisturiser.

Yet astonishingly, her father was right. During Kelly's nine months in the National Guard, she startled herself by unintentionally lasting a day without snorting anything, then two days, four days, a week. Her habit – crucially, her boredom – was interrupted by the 6 a.m. to 9 p.m. schedule of cleaning duties, march drills, rifle instruction, tactical theory classes, artillery workshops, uniform inspections and six-hour hikes lugging a forty-kilogram pack though the Catoctin Mountains, a natural wonder of mud, sandflies and little else.

Finally doing something all day apart from weeping into a pillow and daydreaming about blasting her face off with the Civil War rifle that her father kept in a silver case engraved with the Second Amendment, Kelly couldn't help but recover her health. Much more than she ever achieved with her psychiatrist, Dr Schmidt, who had apparently learnt nothing at Johns Hopkins except how to scribble a Luvox prescription and his weekly invoice. Kelly hated that tanned bald shrink, his soapy voice softened by vacations in the Bahamas and a Lexus coupé financed through his patients' misery. Sometimes she didn't speak a word their entire hour together. Silently they sat in the consultation room, Kelly on the overstuffed Chesterfield doing her nails, Dr Schmidt reading *Newsweek* and texting his son about basketball practice.

But two months at the National Guard barracks and – though she was loath to acknowledge it – Kelly's face glowed a robust pink *without* $175 spent at the organic beauty salon. Exhausted by the dawn wake-ups, her limbs sore from marching drills, Kelly regained an orthodox sleep rhythm; at 11 p.m. she collapsed on her bunk, and, just as she started hankering for her presidential suite of a bedroom back in Georgetown, she drifted off like a drowsy toddler. Her appetite returned too; at dinner she gulped the lukewarm moguls of cheese macaroni swiftly as anyone in the mess hall. Kelly's zigzagging mood hit a temperate plateau, and as her coke-ravaged nostrils recovered their olfactory receptors, she could smell again.

But to whom would she tell the good news? Who cared about her regression from suicide's precipice? Not the other Washington heiresses with whom Kelly once shared beer bongs and quarterbacks at Georgetown frat parties. They weren't *really* her friends. And not the girls she knew up in New York, the catwalk models who coasted their legginess from Midwestern farming towns where they were the tall awkward freaks in school until they blossomed into statuesque yuppies while their classmates got pregnant, got married, got divorced and grilled burgers at Denny's. And not the college track stars Kelly had fucked, before her narcotics eclipsed even the catharsis of sex. If those people knew her story, they'd sell it to the *National Enquirer*.

And nobody in her family, especially her father, would understand Kelly's recovery, nor fathom the magnitude of her near-fatal affliction; not enough to offset their anger that by using drugs, by plotting suicide, she had imperilled the honourable Wesson name. Her older brother Tommy, a carbon copy of his father down to their bullish pink skin, was a semester off graduating law down at Yale. Kelly's real mother, the Miss Texas of 1975, had two toddlers with a trucking tycoon in France. Eight years ago the senator had married Janet LaRoye, a K Street mining lobbyist who was to Kelly a world-class bitch and to everybody else a strawberry blonde bombshell who first earned her conservative stripes as an intern to defence secretary Caspar Weinberger during the invasion of Grenada. In February 2004, during entree at a White House banquet in honour of the Chinese premier, Janet instructed her husband that his promiscuous beauty of a daughter needed strict discipline or else she would inevitably get busted with drugs or fall pregnant, thereby revealing his parental neglect to the Capitol gossip mill.

'Just imagine it, Richard! She'll get snapped on a camera phone snorting something at a frat party. The pictures will reach that prehistoric bitch Barbara Walters. Kelly will fuck up; my gut feeling's *never* wrong. Take my advice. Send the princess into the army. She'll be an officer and play dress-ups.'

The senator – a suspicious man who had fixed policy at the CIA – recognized that his wife wanted Kelly away because her teenage son Dennis would soon return from a detox clinic in Palm Springs. But Richard Wesson had known public life for thirty years and couldn't deny that his party animal of a daughter – with a rumoured coke habit to boot – was a dangerous liability with mid-term elections approaching. So to the barracks she went.

FIFTEEN

Kelly hated the National Guard. She hated everything at the barracks; the shapeless monotone uniforms, the infantilizing nicknames, the drab restrictions on her hairstyle, the she-whale snoring in the bunk beneath her. Most of all, Kelly hated the horny sniggers from virginal crooked-toothed Kentucky farm boys whenever she bent over to pack her bivouac. She couldn't believe that young men so dull and boorish, so irreversibly, unapologetically unstylish, really existed outside of that MTV reality show featuring two socialites slumming it on a Mississippi hog farm. What merciless, sarcastic force had made her fellow recruits so unattractive? *Why?* It was incomprehensible.

Just as unendurable were the weekly 'listen and learn' sessions with other freshmen officers, all of whom had studied hard, voluntarily enlisted, graduated from West Point or Fort Queenscliff and, unlike Kelly, actually gave a shit about the US military. On and on the young officers sucked up to their superiors, on they crapped about respect, honour, discipline, morale, devotion, values, those apple pie words that, Kelly presumed, gave the commanding corporal a throbbing hard-on. Did these young sycophants know another thing she didn't? That by yelling '*yes, sir!*'

or '*immediately sir!*' by puffing out their chests like a randy tomcat, they magically massaged the corporal's prick until he blew in his khakis? No wonder the GI Joes got the best dorms. From what inhuman, emotionless mould, Kelly often wondered during those nine months, had these military men emerged? If, while on the shooting range, she were to blow the sergeant's head off with an M16, would he swiftly be replaced by a flesh and blood doppelganger? Kelly imagined a secret production line, buried deep in a Nevada salt mine controlled by the Pentagon, where pleasureless, obedient men are manufactured from camouflage cotton, sheeps' brains and discarded foreskins. Then into the National Guard they go.

The first month at the barracks, Kelly was desperate to quit. Exhausted, suffering withdrawal symptoms, it was too much. Not just the physical pangs of going cold turkey: stomach cramps, dizziness, hot flushes. It was hatred; the sickening aversion that engorged her. A nauseous reaction to everything at the barracks, erupting within like the sulphur of Hades.

Kelly hated her fellow recruits, hated everything they did *and* didn't do. She hated that the young soldiers regarded everything that her upbringing had taught her to despise – mediocrity obscurity, *ordinariness* – not as cheap shackles but as a safety harness against the heights that famous men fall. She hated that her fellow recruits chortled like hyenas at the feeblest skeleton of a joke, or didn't care for appearances beyond ripped biceps and a crew cut. She hated how they followed the drill sergeant's every word, every damn *thought*, assuming that a mouse on a treadmill existed between that authoritarian bastard's sunburnt ears. She hated how her fellow soldiers relaxed: playing hip-hop CDs at top volume in the rec hall, where they lifted weights, *voluntarily* did sit-ups and called each other dawg or bitch or bro. These beefy high school dropouts, about a third of them white kids and everyone else Hispanic or black, who ceaselessly talked of designer suits, expensive liquor, bling, sportscars with Italian names they couldn't spell, and other luxury items that had always bored Kelly in their meaningless abundance back home.

The white kids were the most frustrating. Kelly hated the remorseless patriotism in these pasty recruits with trailer-park names like Braydon or Randy or Dwayne; she hated their cringeless salutes beneath the flag in the drill yard, their blind respect for the Pentagon puppetmasters deciding their fate like a poker hand. How she despised the young soldiers' obedience to the cowardly bigshots like her own father, who condemn the terrorist prey but never themselves make the kill!

At the root of it, she hated her fellow soldiers' willingness – their presumed *consent* – to get blown up by the Stinger missile launched by a teenage Iraqi wearing a balaclava and imitation Nikes. Kelly hated her fellow recruits, but she didn't want them to die. She wanted to stop these pimply boys who should be in senior year at high school, to break their wings before they took flight as clay pigeons amid the shrapnel smog of Baghdad. She wanted to slap these tough guys in the face, to scream into their ears the truths they didn't know or didn't want to know. To tell the gung-ho military boys about the liars deciding their fate; the stone-hearted warmongers; like her father and his buddies, laughing on the back porch of a mansion in Georgetown. But the young National Guardsmen wouldn't have listened to Kelly Wesson, not a damn word. Because they knew about her.

Somebody at the barracks had made it known that the skinny blonde officer was from *that* Wesson family. Soon everyone knew about her daddy, about her easy ride. At dinner in the mess hall, Kelly pretended to ignore the sneers sent her way. On hikes in the Catoctins, she was allocated the wettest, muddiest, steepest camp site; when her name was called at drills, Kelly heard the sniggers. 'You lazy rich whore!' someone yelled from a truck one morning as she walked to the laundry room. It happened again a few days later.

So the National Guard ensured that suicide never fully disappeared from Kelly's dreams. Not from the dream she'd been having for three years, where she swallowed her dad's gun like an elephantine steel cock and blew her brains out on the US Senate floor, then staggered about, a bloody ghost like Hamlet's father, frothing blood from her temples and staining the plush blue carpet as senators fled, while at the dais the Minotaur calmly resumed his tirade about the North Korean nuclear impasse.

Always, Kelly's splattered head was the dream's most vivid feature; cleaved open like a strawberry chocolate egg, spilling brains, blood, mucous, saliva, all the slippery things that make a person tick . . . and engrossingly detailed too. Never observed an autopsy, never studied anatomy or paid attention in biology class, but somehow Kelly dreamt vividly, realistically, of pink guts, mashed nostrils, exploded arteries. Kelly *felt* her wet dead skull, saw the ruptured capillaries, smelt the ammonia-like whiff of brains on the Senate floor, and then she woke up. Cold sweat beading her forehead, unable to sleep unless she smoked a joint.

That first month at the barracks, the nightmares got worse; redder blood, screams ringing in her ears *after* she awoke, and at 4 a.m., when she badly needed another two hours' sleep before wake-up, Kelly would sneak into the female toilets and stand atop the cistern blowing smoke through a tiny square window.

Kelly thought of gulping all her Valiums at once, of hanging herself with the polyester necktie that she wore on parade duty. That is, until the day she was assigned a post. Suddenly, Kelly was in control of cleaning duty in the mess hall; the lowliest, dullest command position at the barracks. Nevertheless, she was *in charge*. Under Kelly's control were five privates from down south: a bankrupt Mississippian peanut farmer, three black teenagers from Huntsville, Alabama and a Puerto Rican electrical engineer who couldn't find a better job. These men unanimously resented Kelly's orders and wouldn't scour twelve stoves every evening, nor rinse dry spaghetti from three hundred plates that they stacked into dishwashers the width of a garden shed. 'No, lady. We no fucking *sirvientes!*' the Puerto Rican, their unofficial leader, bellowed defiantly when Kelly pointed at the kitchen floor encrusted with stale bolognaise.

She had always shunned household chores herself. Back home on Massachusetts Avenue, a thirty-seven-year-old grandmother from Tijuana cleaned the mansion three times a week. But now that Kelly was in charge, she *wanted* the mess hall clean. She wanted the kitchen floors spotless, the glasses sparkling, the frying pans shiny. Because those were *her* orders, that came from her lips. *Ipso facto*, following the same perversion of logic that compels toddlers to fight over broken toys and men to go to war, Kelly's orders *had* to be followed. But they weren't.

So she began being cruel. Spontaneously, Kelly's viciousness emerged from its gestation commenced three years ago when she started torturing herself in a big silent bedroom overlooking Rock Creek Park. The cruelty wasn't quite intentional, nor was it unexpected; it simply *happened*, her new addiction. Beginning the day Kelly noticed a tingle – a warm, pleasant sensation down in the place that her father's grey dinner guests yearned to touch even if it took them a whole pack of Viagra – while she punished her disobedient inferiors for another lousy cleaning job. Mud beneath the tables, dried soup on the trays, grease coating the stovetops, and again those five lazy soldiers peeled off their rubber gloves and announced that they were done!

Kelly ordered her recruits to stand at attention. No response. The men sat on a kitchen bench, sharing tobacco, reading the sports sections leftover from breakfast. They laughed at the article about a tennis champ who was secretly filmed screwing a prostitute on his day off in Manhattan. The Puerto Rican kicked a scrap of toast that nobody cared to vacuum.

'OK you screw-ups! *I am not impressed!* Look at the floor! Look at the frying pans! This job ain't finished! Nobody is leaving until I'm satisfied. *Nobody!*'

Kelly looked flushed, sick from last night's insomnia. Shouting so loud that even the Mississippi farmer, who'd never actually spoken to his commanding bitch, froze midway through rolling a cigarette. Kelly was shocked too. She hadn't yelled like this since . . . since when? Cheering for the Rangers in the ninth innings with her mother at a ballgame in Houston six years ago? Screaming at the walls the first afternoon she tried to kill herself, tried to pull the trigger, but instead spent five hours weeping, remembering, in her daddy's leather recliner? The soldiers were stunned silent by the tirade erupting from their blonde rake of a commanding officer, like a sonic boom from a golf buggy.

'You fucking dumb lazy cheats! I want this place clean! C-L-E-A-N. Now!'

Murmuring amongst the men. One of the black kids replied softly.

'Yes Ma'am.'

But nobody fetched the mops. Nobody plugged in the vacuum cleaner. They stayed put, sitting on the table.

She's letting off steam. The bitch ain't serious. Probably PMS.

Kelly inhaled, exhaled. Sensing what was to follow Embracing it, perplexed by it.

'You guys won't follow my orders? Run twenty laps around the mess hall. *Now!*'

'*Injusticia!*' the Puerto Rican exclaimed.

'Hell, Ma'am, this ain't no summer camp,' one of the teenagers protested. 'We been doing drills all damn day.'

'If you bastards ignore my orders, I will tell Sergeant Janoski and I will *personally* ensure that you go into the hole,' Kelly spat, making it all up. 'That's solitary confinement in the dark for two weeks!'

One teenager whispered to another. 'They can do that to us?'

'Run the laps or you *will* suffer!'

Slowly, the cleaning team got to their feet. 'Dumb fucking bitch,' the farmer murmured. Then, staring at Kelly through sweat stinging their eyes, the soldiers commenced twenty laps around the musty hall. She wouldn't meet their glares of undisguised hatred, and was careful not to smirk at their humiliation, in case it set off the primal predisposition to killing that made these men so effective at war games.

She couldn't stop quivering, not in the hot cathartic climax of finally teaching the chauvinist bastards a lesson.

A few seconds, there it was. Not precisely an orgasm, but pleasurable as anything that the Georgetown quarterbacks ever achieved down there with their tongues. A curious, staggeringly welcome sensation; not quite penetrative, but akin to a steady, expert caress at *precisely* the right spot. It got better and better, then better still, as she watched her insolent macho subordinates running – *suffering* – in the warm hall. One of the black teenagers limping with his bum knee, all five men fixing Kelly with a look of murder as they jogged by. Nine laps until her panties were wet, and from that lovely moment onwards, she never stopped. If her men showed the slightest trace of insolence, if they didn't address her as Ma'am, if they failed to immaculately polish the ovens, stovetops, grills, or to vacuum every morsel from beneath tables thirty feet long, she punished them mercilessly. And the more explicit their suffering, the better Kelly felt down there.

During those eight months, she forced her five soldiers to run hundreds of laps under the midday sun, to do three-hour march drills, thousands of sit-ups, even to pointlessly lug a three-hundred-pound refrigerator down to the basketball courts and back. And always she savoured the orgasmic tingle. It was addictive; the sensation of Kelly's years of despair, of the powerlessness that had poisoned her like a radioactive cloud, being projected out into these defiant, degraded men where the misery assumed the form of an ephemeral pleasure unit and then glided back inside her, deep inside, to make her come as she watched the soldiers suffering her retribution. They suffered *for* her. And the closer Kelly approached her breathless climax, the crueller she became, until if one of her men merely sniggered they got fifty push-ups on the spot.

Of course, Kelly's sadism made the soldiers more defiant. In late July, one of them – nobody would claim responsibility – forgot to refrigerate a crate of mozzarella. Three days later, seven people came down with food poisoning. As their punishment, Kelly forced her men to scour the latrines with their toothbrushes. The merciless discipline satisfied her not just carnally, but bestowed a pure, inartificial sense of calm that she hadn't known for ten years. Kelly began to acquire the hard stony face of her father (whose features uncannily resembled the monolithic heads on Easter Island). A few adaptations: the sarcastic smirk of his lips, the sharp crest of his eyebrows and though pretty enough for *Vanity Fair's* social pages, Kelly looked more like the Minotaur every day. The meaner she got, the more intoxicated. Unlike the drug habit, Kelly's new addiction *upheld* the law, dispensing the authoritarian jab that her father so cherished.

As she tortured five outspoken, outgunned men, Kelly Wesson enjoyed a blanket of power, of resurrective comfort sans narcotics that she hadn't experienced since she was eleven years old back in Dallas with her mother. With her real mother, a decade ago when her father was merely vice-president of an oil multinational, before his affair and the cover-up, before her mother's ten million dollar pay-off and remarriage to the French trucking magnate who, through paranoid manipulation, kept his wife from seeing her oldest daughter more than once every six months. Watching her soldiers running laps in the yard, Kelly rediscovered the sense of indestructibility, the assumption that nothing could destroy her, that she remembered knowing as she clung to her mother atop their favourite mare Smoky, galloping through brush on their old ranch by the Rio Grande. The fanciful belief indispensible to a happy childhood – *everything will turn out okay* – reappeared reassuringly when Kelly scolded her disobedient men, or, better still, *hurt* them using techniques discretely acceptable to her superiors at the barracks.

'Make a man stand still for a whole afternoon,' the drill sergeant, recently back from Baghdad, advised Kelly during training. 'It breaks him. No water, no pissing. Draw two chalk dots for his feet.'

Immune to the cruelty, she did that too, feeling pleasantly aroused as for four hours her soldiers posed in the yard like a row of bowling pins. She felt just as good watching them scrape dry shit off the toilets or doing two hundred push-ups as punishment for their collective refusal to confess who had yelled 'you crazy slut' when Kelly's back was turned. The giddy cruel catharsis, the carnal euphoria bundled into Daddy's discipline, didn't just render the cocaine in Kelly's toiletries bag less enticing, it saved her.

During nine months of recovery from her bottomless despair, from the drug habit that would have ended in jail, overdose or aneurysm, from the desire not to exist that once hollowed her every breath, Kelly Wesson was resurrected. Resurrected by grinding five decent men into the same powerlessness, the same shit of self-hatred, the same hopeless logic of no exit that compelled her so close to suicide. Did those unfortunate soldiers, enduring their lieutenant's cruel whims for $12.75 an hour, realize that their humiliation fuelled her rebirth? That Kelly got stronger, healthier every day she observed their degradation?

No, they scrubbed the floors, did their sit-ups, ran

their laps, stood like statues under the midday sun. They agreed that Lieutenant Wesson was a mean fucking bitch, obviously spoilt as a kid, and laughed when the peanut farmer from Mississippi explained the sadistic tendencies down to her needing a good, long, old-fashioned fuck in the ass. These men endured her. They endured the same breed of dark instincts that, six thousand miles away, simultaneously possessed the young National Guard reservists guarding Abu Graib. The same cruel, indelibly human impulses that Kelly's father, the Minotaur, employed like a guillotine as he rose through the oil business, the Pentagon and the Senate. Effortlessly, she had become what she hated.

'Forget if the faucets are gold and fuck me.'

It's an order. They embrace on the antique four-poster bed in the master bedroom of her London penthouse. She speaks in a serrated Midwestern drawl, like her father.

Two months out of the National Guard, Kelly Wesson commands a homeless, hunted murderer not to ask dumb questions about the decor and instead stick his dick between her thighs. In many ways she had changed, but in others she remained the same as ever.

And with every direction she writhed, every moan, Max Lamm wordlessly asked the baffling question:

What does she see in you?

It's your otherness, the lure of your transgression. Fuel to the motor of this girl slavishly in thrall to chaos, dysfunction, irredeemable failure; those exotic things in her privileged circles. Of course, she's trying to hurt the megalomaniac father, she wants to destroy him. But his pedigree is her birthmark. *She is what she is.*

Digging into Kelly, into the fertile scarlet grove of this archetypal blonde *shiksa*, Lamm became one of *them*. One of the cumstruck admirers sending her chocolates on Valentine's Day that she threw unopened into the trash. Amid the groping, the sucking, the primal addiction, the sexual act devolved into a hollow glorification of her renovated body, a paean to her moans, a worship of her glistening thighs from afar – though they were inches from his lips – like she was the centrefold in the first porno magazine he ever saw, hidden in the sock drawer belonging to his class-mate Jake Steinberg's father.

'Why are you hiding?' she whispered as Lamm licked the cleft of her navel, then traced her inner thighs with the distal tip of his tongue.

'You killed someone?'

In the absence of his answer, in the exquisite imminence of her release as he found the right spot, Kelly savoured the ambiguity; that her handsome new boy from the barbeque – showered, wearing her father's monogrammed bathrobe and nothing else – could be a dangerous fugitive. A thief or a rapist or a murderer. A stranger, but it's your strangeness that she needs. You're the proxy for her self-destruction.

In this gilded master bedroom, Lamm acceded to her unspoken requests, did what she wanted, what his unthinking urge wanted . . . but he wasn't really there. Was she? Or this was *her* act, a rebellious cathartic act, yet ultimately less than real. London was Kelly's masquerade, her transformation to escape the forces that shaped her: the years contemplating suicide in her luxurious Georgetown bedroom; the daily yearning to blow her brains out with her father's secret gun; the orgasmic sadism in the National Guard that revived her innermost will to live. Returned from suicide's brink, Kelly's recovery was a metamorphosis in reverse, like she'd gone to bed a giant cockroach and woken up a princess.

Yet beneath her skin, nothing had changed. You are what you are.

SIXTEEN

Their first afternoon together. Her bedroom the same as usual. Prada jeans splayed on the carpet, the plasma TV showing a BBC documentary about the chameleons of Madagascar. On the bedside table, unsnorted powder shook to the recoil off his thrusts.

'You don't want any? It's fun.'

She cut a line on the chrome coffee table.

'No. I already can't sleep.'

Lamm answered from the kitchen. She had offered him lunch. The refrigerator a chrome behemoth suited to the galley of a five-star ocean liner. Inside was a thousand quid worth of food: salmon steaks, oysters, cartons of marinated tomatoes, olives, artichokes, peppers, dolmades, mushrooms. The next shelf down: capers, preserved lemons at seven pounds a pot, baguettes, focaccias, linseed rye, three bowls of gnocchi beneath plastic wrap. Dom Pérignon, Château d'Yquem, chardonnay, three six-packs of Belgian beer. And American food too: hot dogs, coleslaw, chilli con carné, cooked fries.

'Look at this! Is Louis the Fourteenth coming for dinner?'

A £20 note stuck up her right nostril, Kelly's voice was ridiculously nasal.

'Maybe. I don't know him. The maid brought that stuff today. Eat what you want.'

Lamm opened the freezer. Among the vodka and water-melon sorbet, there was Kelly's sustenance. Eight boxes of Weight Watchers microwave pizza.

Lamm hadn't felt so hungry since the nightmare night of Malik's death. He sliced a baguette the length of his forearm, cramming its soft trunk with mushrooms, sundried tomatoes, zucchini, pickles, a spread of seeded mustard. He took a beer from the cooler, the same type of bottle that he'd smashed on the teenager's skull. Lamm replaced it and grabbed a Pilsner instead.

'This is *good*.' Kelly's ecstatic exhalation. She knelt by the Philippe Starck coffee table, snorting powder from a groove probably designed for that purpose.

'When did you get into that stuff?'

Fascinating, these pricey powders. He'd seen cocaine in Lagaya's brothel, but never indulged. He was an athlete then; one snort and he'd have failed the urine test. A lot of good the caution did him.

'Oh, when I was, maybe, sixteen. Nothing better to do in DC. I stopped for six months while I was in the National Guard. Then a sergeant got back from destroying plantations in Columbia, and he had *bags* of the stuff. Got me hooked again.'

From her expensively tattered handbag, Kelly removed a credit card. A Visa of some ultra-exclusive mineral: diamond, platinum, double-diamond double-platinum. The card announced: *sell this person whatever the hell they want*. She cut a dot of powder with the Visa's edge, making two lines the length of a matchstick. The remnant she scooped onto a moist fingertip and speckled on her gums.

'My last week in the Guard, the sergeant threw a party at a hotel room in Bethesda. He blew some coke up my ass with a straw. It is *the* most amazing high.'

Kelly unrolled the £20 note, wiping her nose for leftovers.

'How about turning down the TV, Mr Mystery? Let's talk.'

Afterwards, they lay on the four-poster bed. Upon the mantelpiece, Senator Wesson smiled like a Halloween pumpkin.

'Yes, he's my father. Don't give me a fucking sermon about Iraq. Back home, I get one, like, every time I go *anywhere*.'

Lamm blinked. His own father was floating above the bed. Face red, moustache quivering. Again wearing the salmon-pink tennis shirt, white shorts, white sneakers, brandishing a tennis racquet with the Star of David stencilled on its strings.

'Max, you follow this *meshuggeneh* to her apartment. You risk *everything*! What's worse, she's the daughter of Richard Wesson! The Klan's bosom buddy, the next Republican arsehole president! You're the *Jew* who's fucking Richard Wesson's crazy daughter in his own bedroom! If the Muslims don't murder you, the CIA will! And you didn't tell her that you're Jewish, I'll bet she's a closet anti-Semite like her old man!'

The indelible need for a ritual. For '*closure*'; the word beloved by TV anchormen when they report national tragedies. Lamm couldn't ignore Malik Massawi's spectre in the newspapers, on the radio, in Hyde Park's shadows and shimmering back of his eyelids when he tried in vain to sleep.

The indispensible need to repent. *That's* what keeps you awake, that summons your living Father's ghost. Repent to whom? Yourself? The disorder, degeneration, delirium essential to a nervous breakdown; it drove through the weedy entrance to Lamm's memory and neglected to shut the gate. His mad yearning to atone for a murderous misdeed, to satisfy the strange outpouring of guilt that, millennia by millennia, has fuelled the confessional fire at the crux of the great religions. Contrary to the newspapers, you're no psychopath. But somehow you *need* to say sorry, to cleanse yourself. Your conscience draws you to God. Your conscience is God?

Tomorrow morning – a Saturday – you will go to that synagogue on Great Cumberland Street.

For the dead boy, you'll recite *kaddish*. The ancient Jewish prayer for the dead. Is it acceptable to say *kaddish* for a Muslim? Don't tell the rabbi.

The Western Marble Arch synagogue. Probably the capital's most distinguished congregation, with its mumbling rows of judges, QCs, assorted medical specialists, prominent businessmen and their children studying for their parents' professions. Men on the ground floor, women up top. The regular pulpit of the Chief Rabbi, Baron Jonathan Sacks, who earlier that week had co-authored the multifaith condemnation against the Camden Hate Killer. On the bus, Lamm had often passed that grand temple guarded by two Israeli security men at the door. But he'd never gone inside.

During his schooldays at Mount Scopus Memorial College, Lamm wasn't particularly observant. Nor were his classmates, except the Religious Zionist kids who wore knitted yarmulkes, scored the best grades and on Friday nights drank enough kosher wine to fell the Pharaoh's most fearsome slavedriver. After seven years of Hebrew classes, Lamm knew four words (apart from the mandatory blessings). *Ken, lo, kelev, kisev.* Yes, no, dog, money. Four words in a peerlessly ancient language that sounds like clearing your throat. The Hebrew teachers were young Israeli women just out of National Service. Tough leather-faced *sabras* who could dispatch you with their bare hands. At this Jewish school, like most of the others, synagogue was primarily a social event. Every Saturday morning, two hours of gossiping, making faces at the girls upstairs, or sticking witty notes – e.g. I EAT POO – on the back of the boy in front of you.

Confused, contrary Lamm! Suddenly he felt this unfamiliar urge: *go to the synagogue this Saturday.* Visit synagogue to say the memorial *kaddish* prayer, and not for your late grandmother Alma Lippmann who scented your childhood with baked *rougelach*, not for great-uncle Harry who died from a botched triple-bypass on the operating table, but for the Pakistani teenager that you dispatched with an empty beer bottle.

Lamm's Day of Atonement had arrived six months early, although he had never really observed Yom Kippur. That one day a year when nearly all Jewish families go to synagogue, even the irreligious ones. The day the synagogue seats are reconfigured to accommodate the High Holidays crowds. When most Jews neither eat nor drink for twenty-five hours, but *schmooze* when they should be praying, then during the closing minutes of the final *ne'ila* service they repent for another year of pointlessly arguing with their children/spouses/parents/

siblings, of giving too little to charity, of seldom visiting great-uncle Eugene at the nursing home, of anonymously driving away from the parked Saab they reversed into, of sometimes being selfish, rancorous, mendacious, spiteful, untrustworthy . . . Together, the Jews repent for a year of being a human being. Then within a day, sometimes an hour if the family starts arguing at the dinner table, most everybody gets back to the morally imperfect zigzag of day-to-day life. Every Jew makes mistakes, but not like Max Lamm.

And if you don't visit the synagogue to repent for Malik's death? A lightning bolt will strike you down? Spectres of guilt will invade your dreams, as Jacob saw angels ascend his ladder while he slept upon a rock at Mount Moriah? Will you see portents of your destruction, as did the Pharaoh, who dreamt of the seven lean cows that rose from the river and devoured seven fat cows, and seven withered ears of grain that devoured seven fat ears? Tired, tortured Lamm! The thoughts of divine retribution, of a worse catastrophe inflamed by his guilt, were, of course, what the vehement opponent of religious atonement – communist, Satanist, atheist – would dismiss as pious paranoia, mumbo jumbo, a fairytale of self-doubt.

But Lamm had already decided: tomorrow morning, you will visit the synagogue to recite *kaddish* for Malik Massawi. Might this prayer of repentance offer intangible peace? You'll be doing *something*. You can't visit the boy's family to apologize for killing their son. You can't bring him back. So you *will* recite the Jewish prayer for the dead, the ancient prayer that even the don't-give-a-fuck-about-being-Jewish Jews, the trendy young ones contemptuous of their heritage, *still* mumble over the death of a loved one. Malik wasn't Jewish, but *you killed him*. That boy was the future, now he's a slab of cold flesh devoid of anything but the past.

SEVENTEEN

Saturday 9 April

All along Great Cumberland Street, Lamm was haunted by the ghosts of why. His proximity to a synagogue so unnerving. He'd evaded Jewish life, swathed in his repellent of one part cynicism, three parts disgrace. Now, a failure, he was *voluntarily* visiting a congregation. Not being born-again, not a Jewish version of Bob Dylan's *meshuggeneh* conversion to Christianity when he saw a cross glistening in the crowd at a rock arena. Lamm was attending a *minyan* of ten Jewish men, simply to atone. He'd long thought himself too smart for rituals, traditions, ancient law, 'spirituality'. And where's being so clever got you? Ten thousand pounds on your head. A grease trap for a home.

He crossed Seymour Street to the synagogue entrance. Hesitation scrambled his resolve. Enough! Walk through the fucking door!

A hunched grey figure shuffled inside. Eighty-five years old in a woollen overcoat, two hearing aids beneath a frayed fedora. The old man smiled, genuine as any greeting Lamm had ever received.

'*Shabbat Shalom.* We're both running late!'

Spontaneously, Lamm laughed. Tried to stop himself.

Not now, on the way to saying *kaddish* for the boy you recently killed. The security guards might suspect that you're a madman terrorist, giggling about the nail bomb you hid beneath the kosher buffet. Still, he kept laughing and in a moment strange as anything yet in the strangest week of his life, Lamm stopped in the circular driveway, beneath the statue of Raoul Wallenberg the righteous gentile, and he let it all out. Quietly laughing at everything; the oily tennis shoes cladding his sponsorless feet, his heated hovel beneath a hotplate, the famous senator's blonde nymphomaniac daughter he'd just fucked, the hairy Iranian barber in Queensway who sold genuine wigs and fake passports, the riot-fuelled hysteria in the *Sun* as accurate as soothsaying from the guts of a rabbit, the police searching for a neo-Nazi murderer when you, the culprit, are the maternal grandson of Alma Weinraub who survived Auschwitz, the old man who just wished you *Shabbat Shalom* like you're a regular at this synagogue. Out trickled Lamm's hoarse laugh, dripping from the well-spring of humanity, of resilience, of a great fuck-you to the unforeseen, that wells within us and doesn't disappear until our final breath.

Lamm caught his reflection in a glass pane embossed with the Star of David. Not bad; you look halfway respectable. You're not carrying a suspicious backpack. Bareheaded, but they should let you in. A few congregants passed by, running late. These respectable Jews with their tallit bags and whingeing kids! Exemplars of order with clean soft hands facilitated by their day job at the surgery or the law chambers or the accountancy practice, with *siddurim* stacked in the wooden box beneath their member's plaque and atop their heads yarmulkes monogrammed with their initials. A big crowd; must be a bar mitzvah today. Remembering that he hadn't eaten breakfast, Lamm envisaged the *Kiddush* that would follow the service. All that deli food! Pickles, falafels, *hatzolim* dip, blintzes, latkes, *kugelhopf*, fresh sweet *challa* that you haven't tasted in years. Good thing your jacket's got big pockets. Swiftly the hunger cleaved his gut, up his throat; the impossible feeling to shake.

At the door, Lamm spoke to the taller of the two security guards. A young Sephardi, just out of his mandatory two years in the Israeli army. The guard wore a numbered badge: ALON BEN-DAVID NO. 253.

'*Shabbat Shalom*,' Lamm offered.

In the guard's thick accent, the bludgeoning question. 'You been here before?'

'First time.'

'Where you from?'

'Australia.'

The guard noticed Lamm's dusty hair, greasy pants, scuffed shoes. The clues in this young stranger's eyes: shadowy circles, premature lines, bloodshot pink whites hollowed into a poorly shaven face. Probably slept in the park last night. He wants the free food. But there was something else, something creepily engaging about this shabby visitor claiming to be a citizen of the Commonwealth. His desperate gaze, silently disturbing as anything the guard saw during his three years in an IDF reconnaissance unit when he'd stared into the remorseless eyes of foiled suicide bombers at a Gaza jail full of unsuccessful terrorists, or seen the bodies of Hamas riflemen spilling guts beneath tanks in the territories, Palestinian children wearing mock suicide belts at a parade in the Jenin refugee camp, or the gruesome remnants of the 2002 suicide bombing that killed thirty Jews at a Passover Seder in Netanya. This tough, world-weary guard was disturbed by Max Lamm, enough to prolong the interrogation.

'Why you here?'

'To say *kaddish*.'

'*Why?*'

Good question. *Why?* Funny, how useless trivia resurfaces at your most dangerous moments. Lamm recalled the answer that Edmund Hillary famously gave to a journalist who asked why he'd conquered Mt Everest. *Because it's there.*

'Because I should.'

The guard removed his sunglasses, staring at the stranger. 'My father died last week,' Lamm added. 'I'm saying *kaddish* for him.'

'What's your Hebrew name?'

'Gedalya BenYehuda.'

The guard frisked Lamm, then opened the door.

'Sorry, extra security because of the riot. We had a bomb threat yesterday.'

The *Jewish News* was stacked in a pile by the door. Lamm read the front page headline:

CAMDEN MURDER PROVOKES ANTI-SEMITIC ATTACKS IN HENDON, GOLDERS GREEN

The guard handed Lamm a black yarmulke.

'Go to your right. The service has begun.'

Rachel Samuels. Her rusty auburn hair, aqua-green eyes so rare for a Jewish girl. Unfailingly, inartificially luminescent, never plastered in make-up. This girl whose fantastic unclothed possibilities, fuel and fire to the hormonal upheaval in her pubescent admirers, were imagined by Lamm most nights of his twelfth year. Alone in bed beneath his *Star Wars* blankets, he'd envisage the magical moment – his triumph – when finally they'd kiss. You'll do it on school camp? At this weekend's sleepover? At Rachel's thirteenth birthday party? For a year, her birthday invitation remained pinned on Lamm's cupboard, his beacon.

Unlike his older friends in ninth grade, Lamm rarely imagined going all the way with Rachel. The other boys loved to envisage her deflowerment: those glistening amber shoulders, precocious perfect breasts, legs akimbo gleaming their hypnotic chocolate sheen. Invariably, the boys hardened up when she walked through the school canteen. Their favourite discussion topics: who's kissed her? Who's fingered her? Who's humped her? Rachel Samuels watered the wet dreams of nearly all the eighth- and ninth-grade boys at Mount Scopus College.

Then, one unseasonally cold Wednesday in December 1988, she flew to New York after visiting her brother in London. Thirty-eight minutes after take-off, Rachel was blown out of the aircraft at 31,000 feet when a Samsonite briefcase exploded in the left flank or the fuselage. Almost two minutes later, she landed in a fallow tract near the village of Tundergarth, a few miles outside Lockerbie in the southern fields of Scotland.

And nobody ever learnt that on the last night of first semester, 1988, Max Lamm *had* kissed her. Briefly – but on the lips! – in the moonlit schoolyard during the intermission of *Fiddler on the Roof*, the school musical that year. First day back at class, Lamm would have told his friends the triumphant news. Would've been the thirteen-year-old king of the schoolyard. But he didn't tell anyone, not when the school was engulfed by the stark indelible shock of Rachel Samuels' famous death. Lockerbie was, up to that point, the worst terrorist attack ever perpetrated against the United States: 259 passengers and crew killed when about 450 grams of Semtex plastic explosive detonated in a luggage container. Within ten seconds, according to the flight investigators, the 747's cockpit, fuselage and wings were plummeting separately. The wing section – containing 91,000 kilograms of jet fuel – crashed into a street called Sherwood Crescent, causing a seismic event measuring 1.6 on the Richter scale. Two families and an entire block of houses were vaporised into a crater forty-seven metres long.

And Rachel Samuels – *his* Rachel Samuels – sat in seat 3A on that airliner. After her brother told him, Lamm never forgot her seat number. Even now, sixteen years on, if he saw a word containing three As – aardvark, Arkansas, caravan – her exquisite spectre returned, together with the lump in his throat. Rachel's playful voice in his ear, asking when he would kiss her again.

For six months, Lamm didn't touch a tennis racquet. The coach gave up calling, his parents tried and failed. Wouldn't leave his bedroom except for school or the library to do research into the bombing. Lamm was obsessed by anything, *everything* about the crime. The FAA investigation, the FBI investigation, the conspiracy theories, the lucky ones who missed the flight. The millisecond, that otherwise ordinary instant, when the suitcase bomb detonated and its supersonic shockwaves ruptured the cockpit's bulkhead wall. The type of timer the bombmaker used; a precision piece manufactured by Mebo, a Swiss firm that exported to Libya. And Lamm's unforgettable imagining of the fuselage roof peeling back, tornado-strength winds ripping into the cabin, transforming untethered items – trolleys, cups, cutlery – into lethal flying objects. Rachel's final moments. Was she conscious? Did she absurdly, fleetingly, think of *you*? Or the sudden drop in atmospheric pressure collapsed Rachel's lungs, as the experts suggested had occurred to the victims, so she'd already blacked out when the 747's nose section hit the moors. Apparently, an airline steward and a male passenger were found alive near the cockpit door, but succumbed before the ambulances arrived. Lamm's eternal engrossing question: *what was it really like?*

And the conspiracy theories! Only a month's mourning, a month's obsession, until Lamm – a thirteen-year-old bar mitzvah boy who had, up to that point, never memorized anything more complicated than his multiplication tables – knew the mysterious details by heart:

1. Four CIA agents were victims on Pan Am 103. One of them, Major Charles McKee, had been in Beirut trying to locate the American hostages kidnapped by Hezbollah. In a Lockerbie field, a police dog handler found McKee's scorched briefcase. It contained classified maps of terrorist hideouts in Lebanon. Witnesses reported seeing American agents removing documents from the briefcase, then re-planting it for 'discovery' by Scottish constables.

2. The South African foreign minister, Pik Botha, was booked on Pan Am 103. He was en route to New York for the signing of a treaty relinquishing control of Namibia to the United Nations. A few hours before take-off, the South African delegation changed their booking. But the UN Ambassador to Namibia, Bernt Carlsson – who organized the Namibia treaty against South African opposition – died aboard Pan Am 103. A British diplomat, Patrick Heseldine,

petitioned the UN to investigate whether the apartheid regime had plotted the bombing.

3. Juval Aviv, an ex-Mossad officer employed as lead investigator for Pan Am airlines, claimed that the CIA ran a protected drug route from Europe to the United States. Codenamed Operation Corea, allegedly the CIA permitted the Syrian drug dealer Monzer al-Kassar to smuggle heroin on Pan Am flights, in exchange for intelligence on Palestinian terrorist groups. But on 21 December, 1988, so the theory claimed, terrorists swapped the contraband suitcases: one containing drugs for one containing a bomb.

Lamm gorged himself on the bombing's facts, figures, conspiracy theories. In his bed in the dark, there was Rachel plummeting thirty-thousand feet, aflame in her flight slippers. Her exquisite face gazing down, down, down to the end. Finally one morning in February 1989, following a typically sleepless night of watching Rachel burning amid the glare of his desk lamp, Lamm stopped the spiral. The lightning bolt of common sense; cease the fixation on her death, or you *will* destroy yourself as mercilessly as the bombers destroyed that airliner. Iran, Syria, Libya, Hezbollah, the PLO or South Africa; whoever is the culprit, they won't suffer justice. They've got impunity in their state sponsors, their black gold or gold gold. Fuck them. *Move on.*

To the relief of his parents, teachers, coaches and friends, Lamm stopped buying the *Journal of the National Military Intelligence Association* at a military book stall in the Camberwell Market, stopped cutting clippings of every Pan Am 103 investigation published in the newspapers, stopped subscribing to newsletters sent by a dozen crank conspiracy theorists. Rachel Samuels – *his* Rachel Samuels – wasn't coming back. The excruciating truth: she's gone.

Hungry, haunted Lamm! In the hole beneath Hyde Park, he couldn't stop yearning for agnostic redemption from his crime. But now, in the Western Marble Arch synagogue reciting *kaddish* with the rabbi and ninety-seven respectable Jews, *Rachel's* was the face visiting him. Not Malik's, but Rachel's! Venus charred in the jet fuel flames, mourned like she fell from the sky not seventeen years ago, but yesterday. It was Lamm's recollection of the girl that he still tried not to love, that he tried to forget – *not* the memory of the Pakistani boy that he'd bludgeoned to death – that compelled him to remain in this grand synagogue of oak benches, silver lamps and marble corridors, to keep listening, reciting, remembering. He had to stay through the Torah portion, through the *aliyahs*, until the rabbi invited the congregation's mourners to recite the *kaddish* memorial for the recently deceased.

> *Yitgaddal v'yitqaddash sh'meh rabba, B'al'ma di v'ra khiruteh v'yamlikh malkhuteh . . .*

Lamm mumbled these sacred words for Rachel Samuels, whose soft fulsome lips he imagined the Hebrew verses streaming into. *Kaddish*, the ancient hymn of mourning, of praise, of exultation that every observant Jew knows by heart, that announces always the same bleak truth; a Jew has died. The prayer missed Malik Massawi's corpse, flying from Lamm's lips into his memory of Rachel Samuels the night he kissed her, into the bewitching green eyes that were his adolescent lifeblood until the day she fell to earth.

> *. . . itbarakh v'yishtabbach v'yitpaar v'yitromam*
> *v'yitnasse v'yithaddar v'yitalle v'yithalla*
> *sh'meh d'qudsha . . .*

Not merely saying *kaddish*, but *praying* it for the first time since . . . ever? You love her more than ever, but she won't return. Seventeen years is a day.

Here in this synagogue, come back!

Be the girl that enraptured me! Whom I love endlessly, unconditionally.

For one day!

Soon you'll be in that box. The barbeque hole is a rehearsal for your grave. If Malik's avengers don't hunt you down, if the police don't get you, if the *Daily Mail* doesn't publicly castrate you, if a tattooed Neanderthal in prison doesn't strangle you because you won't suck him off, then you'll die from the memories of her. This bottomless serpentine haze of anchorless voices, fragments of embraces, fimbriae of long-gone encounters, merciless sleeplessness, black wet grass, unimaginably distant stars mocking you through the barbeque's grille, all beaten into the enlivened nightmarish pulp of your crime, your failure, your disgrace, your life, your death and what's the difference anyway?

Enough. Do it. Jump off the gherkin-shaped tower on St Mary Axe. It's foolproof, there's a nice view at the end. The Americans have the stiff Washington monument for fucking the world, the Brits have an unerect cucumber. The tabloids will love it. *Racist Jewish Murderer Jumps to Death off Gherkin.* They'll throw cucumbers on your gravestone.

Following *kaddish*, the cantor sang a Hebrew psalm in his magnificent rich voice. A psalm written by King David three thousand years ago. The congregation chatted about the weather, the business, the family, the race riots, the upcoming holiday to Majorca or the Great Barrier Reef. The mourner's prayer had concluded so swiftly and Lamm had missed most of it! Too hypnotized by Rachel's spectre, he hadn't even opened the prayer book!

Her ghost was in the synagogue. Thirteen years old, Rachel stood on the *bima* in her Mount Scopus College uniform. Eyes unforgettably aqua-green, hair shimmering shoulder-length, a thumb poking through the hole in the right sleeve of her sweater. In the moonlit schoolyard, she smiled shyly as Lamm brought his lips to hers. Never had her cherubic face appeared this excruciatingly perfect. The girl that obsessed him the instant they met eighteen years ago.

Like Mr Lewski in the park, Rachel was silent. Not a word.

Talk to me!

Rachel!

Lamm blinked. She was gone.

EIGHTEEN

Lamm's under-15s doubles partner, Joshua Berkoff, told him the story of his Uncle Solly who went to the madhouse. For decades a force of efficiency: a *macher* in the community, a champion in the Maccabi squash league, the owner of a successful chain of jewellery stores. Then Solly's life came apart like a necklace in two. A nervous breakdown was the official line but, Berkoff confided, in truth his uncle admitted to have seen the ghost of his dead mother hovering above the bed whenever he fucked the *shiksa* mistress.

Our ghosts drop in for our mistakes. Madness, sin, catastrophe. Then – like Mr Lewski in Hyde Park or Rachel Samuels in the Western Marble Arch synagogue – they suddenly depart, doing French kicks in a conga line through the invisible curtain between life and death. Dancing off-stage without saying a thing.

Rachel's ghost – Lamm's hallucination? – had departed. So had everybody. The synagogue empty, the crowd was in the adjacent hall for the bar mitzvah boy's celebratory *Kiddush*. Hungry, Lamm followed the marble corridor into a large carpeted room adorned by a watercolour canvas of Moses gazing wistfully across the border of Canaan at the Promised Land forbidden to him. Probably a hundred people in here; the regular congregants in white shirts or sensible blouses, the bar mitzvah invitees overdressed in pinstriped suits or their finest dresses. Nobody noticed Lamm's dusty shoes and greasy pants, or they pretended not to. At the door, the guests were greeted by a slim grey man wearing horn-rimmed glasses.

'First time at our synagogue?' he inquired in clipped Oxford vowels.

'It is.'

'My name's Arnold. Dr Arnold Fraid. Perhaps we'll see you during the week? We always need an extra *minyan* man. Do enjoy the food, it appears that you need it.'

Lamm waited by the curtains as the rabbi made the *Hamotzi* blessing over the challah. The bar mitzvah boy was a fat little maths whiz named Robbie Zerman, who had read his Hebrew *parsha* in a high-pitched lilt suggesting that puberty was still a few months off. His beaming parents had stood beside him, white knuckles clasped together. Similarly chubby, the mother a psychologist at the LSE and the father a computer hotshot who, the rabbi informed the congregation, was working on the next Google. The rabbi, Baum, was a fortysomething beanpole with a sideshow salesman's voice, a thin beard and a newsreader's mat of black hair. Had he not elected to serve the faith, he would've excelled as a radio-miked salesman in a shopping mall. Would've sold a hundred vacuum cleaners a week to bored housewives in Staines, but Baum passed up Amway's bonuses to bury elderly congregants and put rocks on their gravestones, to lecture bar mitzvah boys on how not to sound ungrateful in their big speech, to teach first-timers at the communal Seder the hows and whys of Passover. The rabbi shook Lamm's hand like a bottle of ketchup.

'*Good Shabbos!* Wonderful to see you today!'

Good for him, Lamm decided. A grip like a plumber's wrench, hair like a yak, he's hawking Maimonides' wisdom instead of a free set of steak knives. We should all be so lucky.

And look at this spread! A kosher deli sponsored by the bar mitzvah boy's parents. Half a bowl of thick hummus and pickles lathered upon crackers, and Lamm started to feel better. Between mouthfuls, he checked out the congregation. The guests flocked to Robbie Zerman, the little hero. The usual avalanche of royal blue ties, bouffant perms, tallit clips, Manchester United yarmulkes, handshakes, hugs, kisses. Not so interested in the food. The overdressed guests nibbled a carrot stick, dipped a biscuit, but what they liked was talking. Shiny women hugging, air-kissing, comparing hats, laughing about their love handles and their beautiful smart daughters holidaying on a Spanish beach.

Lamm hadn't ever felt so at home, so far away from home. Yet to these people, he was the invader from another world: Planet Disorder. Look at these Jews. Lawyers, dentists, physicians, brokers, bigwigs in the rag trade. A few academics and writers at the shallower end of the income ramp. Sixty years ago their parents, famished behind barbed wire, would have jumped from their skin at a spread like this! Would've thanked Hashem as they wolfed down the fish balls. And, true to form, only the guests old enough to be survivors – the grey-haired, liver-spotted eaters tough as tough *alte kockers* are – were the ones eating with gusto. Lamm observed the quintessential habit of Jews who had evaded starvation in the ghettos or Hitler's camps, as he watched an elderly man carefully wrap two fillets of fried fish into a napkin, then stuff the oily bundle into his jacket packet.

The buffet was keenly attended by octogenarian men wearing fifty-year-old herringbone suits, polishing off the herring as their wives consumed fish balls, cheesy blintzes and garlic eggplant dip, then kissed the gagging bar mitzvah boy. Multiple generations of hard-working Jewish families and the murderer Max Lamm, in the one room. This *Yiddishkeit* universe that you're missing! The bar mitzvah boy's school friends wearing bands on their teeth and nice new suits, so dull yet respectable compared to a force of degenerate cumhappy excess like yourself. Look at their older brothers, halfway through university. Can these Jewish boys be any different? Why join the Pakistanis rioting in Bethnal Green? Why organize sit-ins against an unjust war, as their parents did, and risk getting expelled? These days, you won't get back in. The young men have what they're told they need: a commerce degree at King's College or Cambridge, nice shoes, fresh sushi, cable TV, a cute Citrôen hatchback.

Fuck risking it! say the silk ties, the easy smiles of these Jewish boys five years younger than you, who have jobs lined up building the houses of cards at Deutsche Bank, Morgan Stanley, Merrill Lynch. Fuck dropping out to ride with Abbie Hoffman, fuck Allen Ginsberg, fuck the Mahavishnu Orchestra, fuck acid parties and ashrams. Fuck whatever their parents did before law school beckoned. Fuck Paris in May '68, fuck demonstrating against the mini-My Lai that's perpetrated every other day in Iraq. Fuck taking to the streets with homemade banners. That's for Muslims in the East End or the French who don't know better. Who dodges Molotov cocktails in a good suit? Let Hollywood stars make political protests, they can afford to. Not the smiley Jewish twentysomethings here, talking business at a buffet they're too content to eat. They're making deals, meeting the right girl, working towards a Lexus or else a BMW if they don't object to driving a German car, and they don't. The Shoah was sixty years ago. An eternity! On the twenty-fifth floor of a Fortune 500 skyscraper, their *goyishe* friends have barely heard of Auschwitz.

Decrepit, doomed Lamm! No, he wasn't hateful watching these Nice Jewish Boys – merely mystified by their unanimous grins, their relaxation, their apparent absence of guilt, desperation, sexual dysfunction, madness . . . all the things that make life interesting. What obsesses these eligible Jewish men, if not your silent ghosts and dead voices? Italian loafers, tennis on Sundays, showers twice a day, exams for the Bar, two-storey homes overlooking Hampstead Heath. A golden retriever and a pretty girl just like them.

A ghost. At the buffet table sat Lamm's grandfather, Abram Moshinsky. Deceased three years ago aged eighty-nine, he wore his tweed hat, mothballed Brooks Brothers suit and a cream-coloured *tallit* with its fringes dangling to the floor. He studied the grey slivers of herring, like a jeweller examining gems, picking the best ones and piling them upon a slice of challa. Staring at Lamm, Abram Moshinsky's face eroded beneath his white beard. A Flinders Lane shirt-maker for thirty-seven years, from the week he arrived from Poland in 1946 until his retirement, he was nevertheless a learned man who had learnt the Tanakh, the Talmud, some Kaballah, the books of Prophets. In Buchenwald he shared a bare bunk with a genius of a yeshivah student who knew entire tracts of Talmud by heart, who recited *tehillim* from memory until the black moment, only a month before liberation, when he succumbed to typhus while whispering the *Shema Yisrael* into the night.

His grandfather's favourite passages of the Tanakh, Lamm remembered from long-ago discussions at the Friday-night dinner table, wasn't the salvation joyfully celebrated in the Book of Esther or the Song of Songs. Instead, Abram Moshinsky loved those verses evoking his own slavery under the German pharaohs. The lyrical evocation of destruction, desolation and doom recounted in *Eikhah*, the book of Lamentations. That ancient book read on the ninth day of the Hebrew month of Av, when observant Jews don't eat or drink for twenty-five hours, don't shower or wash their hands past the knuckles, and sit on the bare floor reading Jeremiah's account of Jerusalem's rape, pillage, downfall. A mourning not only of the holy Temple's devastation by the Babylonians in 589 BC, but the litany of genocidal sorrows that have afflicted the Jewish people ever since.

Lamm's grandfather pushed aside his plate, gathering his *tallit* fringes in his shaking right hand. His face craggy and hard, he shouted above the noisy guests.

'Max, you listen to me! For three and a half thousand years we have been punished! Again and again and again! Punished for disrespecting each other, for being arrogant before our Maker, for speaking *loshon hora* about our fellow Jews, for caring more about wealth and luxury than each other, for spending our pay on *tchotchkes* instead of the hungry family on the street! *That* is why we lost Yerushalem! *That* is why our Temple fell, may it be rebuilt! We punish ourselves!'

Lamm blinked. The platter of herring was identical as before.

The Jewish twentysomethings chatted, laughed, removed their yarmulkes and checked their mobile phones. Lamm asked himself: do these young Jewish supermen realize the historical singularity of their good fortune? The well-dressed bachelors gossiping at the buffet, itching to escape this stuffy hall and go shopping on Oxford Street, will be successes in a Europe curiously devoid of genocidal Romans, Cossacks and Nazis, a Europe devoid of crusaders massacring barnfuls of Jews, of popes demanding conversion or death for the Christ-killers, of pogrom propagandists proclaiming that the Jews use Christian children's blood for making the Passover matzah, of Polish peasants burning synagogues and two hundred years later the *Einsatzgruppen* behind the Eastern Front . . . the incredible horrors that were, until recently, the mainstay of Jewish existence upon this scorched continent. Lamm noticed a brass plaque set above the front door, proclaiming that the Western Marble Arch synagogue was founded in 1761. When Europe's guilds and universities demanded that the ambitious Jew be baptized or else grow turnips his entire life. Listen to these privileged Jewish boys who ignore the buffet. Discussing their cars, their clothes, their exciting financial jobs in the City.

'What good is contentment without hunger?'

Max Lamm whispered to himself, to the vanished ghost of his grandfather who for fifty-seven years lit *Yartzheit* candles for his sisters who starved to death at Bergen-Belsen. Finally the fugitive awoke to his senses. Embrace the bonanza! Falafel balls, four kinds of sponge cake, tahini, potato latkes with olive relish . . . no wonder the guards questioned you. Lamm was wrapping five blintzes into a napkin when somebody tapped his shoulder.

'*Hoongry this morningk?*'

An Eastern European accent. Czech, or Hungarian? The voice of a dastardly TV spy from behind the Iron Curtain.

Staring at Lamm was the *shammas*, the synagogue volunteer who guides mourners to the ark, locates seats for latecomers, helps disabled visitors, packs away the prayer books. A gaunt bearded stick with white fluff up-top, a prickly snow beard and thick glasses. Looked seventy-five from his thousands of hours studying Torah in *a Kolel*, but probably twenty years younger than that.

'Nobody eat zis food, it gets bad. Take it home.'

He pushed a bowl of avocado dip into Lamm's hands.

'My name is Eli Kohn.'

'I'm George.'

'*Shabbat Shalom*, George.' The *shammas* drew his breath.

'Are you sleeping in ze park?'

Glaring into Lamm's pupils, at the truth, Eli chewed a pickle. The fugitive was stunned.

'I'm staying in a flat on Queensborough Terrace.'

'You're not sleeping under ze barbeque?'

Nobody here *looked* like an undercover cop. Too old, too young, too chatty, too soft. The *shammas* peered at Lamm's jeans.

'Your trousers have dust. It's iron oxide and calcium carbonate from ze old barbeque in Hyde Park. I do not forget ze colour. I used to cook a fish zer wiz my daughter.'

Biscuit snagged in Lamm's throat.

'I vas a geologist for thirty years. Have you been sleeping in ze barbeque? People do.'

A scrap of repentance for inadvertently killing a Pakistani teenager so he might sleep. That's what Lamm wanted. Not this interrogation from a rock expert with the elocution of Dr Strangelove. Eli Kohn peppered Lamm with breath scented by the salmon dip. Definitely no undercover cop, the old Jews from the old country, they all smell like this! How much you've missed! Proust tasted a *petite madeleine* dipped in tea, you sniff a *frum* bearded sleuth marinated in herring. Your descent is complete. With a glance, this *chochem* of a geologist sees what you've become. He recognizes your bottomlessness. You're Esau deprived of his father's birthright, you're Jonah in the belly of the whale.

And you're surprised it feels strange!

But strange things are happening all the time. Later that Saturday afternoon, four days after Max Lamm's catastrophe, they met in the master bedroom. She was pleasured more by the lines of cocaine she'd hoovered up, he suspected, than his dick inside her. Still, if this was his final conquest before twenty years of avoiding randy inmates in the prison shower, so be it.

'*Keep doing that*,' she moaned. And in Kelly's insatiability he felt what? Perverse pride that she chose to fuck him instead of Donald Trump Jr in a Fifth Avenue penthouse? Gratitude, that with her carnal addiction was the five-star daycare centre for a homeless fugitive? Gasping, she pulled him in. This, Lamm presumed, is the way princesses moan on the wedding night of their arranged marriage. They're invigorated not only by the instinctive thrust, by the animal catharsis of seeing your Prince Charming going at it like a dog in heat, but also by hot reprieve from the decorum, pomp, pretence that pervades a royal life – a life not unlike Kelly Wesson's – like a fog.

'Come *now*!' Kelly whispered again. Her spidery amber

legs pirouetted roofwards, engorging him. *Okay*, Lamm decided. He stopped looking at the framed photograph that prolonged his virility, in which Senator Wesson and Newt Gingrich shook hands with North Korea's Dear Leader on a junket to Pyongyang.

'Just a second,' Lamm stammered. Nudging Kelly against the Versace bolster, he found a groove.

'That's *good*,' she murmured. Lamm kept going from behind as she arched her back, oohing melodramatically as he sensed the hint of ejaculation.

He lurched forward, gasping. She presumed it was his climax, the impossibility of containing the wad any longer. But shock was the culprit. Because there, sitting on the pillow by Kelly's right shoulder, was the deceased Pakistani boy. Another ghost in Lamm's kingdom.

Malik Massawi looked as he did the night *it* happened. Red baseball cap, black Nike windbreaker, cheap gold chain around his neck, plastic diamond in his left ear. Blood streaming from his right temple, running its ruby signature of foreclosure down his cheek. Most disturbing were the eyes. Malik's body appeared living, undecayed, but his eyes were horrific. The deep brown pupils shooting that glance of astonishment from the moment the bottle cracked his skull.

Malik Massawi's eyes were bleeding. Not just bleeding, but writhing, swelling, seeping with larvae, fat white worms, maggots. The dead boy's pupils oozed blood, bile, pus, cum, tears. Seeping scarlet chunks, this blood torrent of infection, infarction, infestation slopping down his cheeks onto the bone-white bedspread. Bleeding, ejaculating, shitting out his ghostly eyes, Malik's posthumous excretia stained the sheets and the lovers' naked bodies. The red filth rained onto Kelly's breasts, running a crimson stream into her belly button.

Lamm stared ahead at Malik, at the living dead boy's spiral of fluids dripping upon Kelly's left kneecap. 'Keep going,' she heaved. Mindlessly Lamm re-entered, following orders. It *did* feel good, so good, yet as he fucked harder, closer to the end, his victim's ghost came on stronger. Impossible to ignore. And Malik's spectre didn't say a word; infuriatingly silent like all the others!

'*Harder!*' she gasped. Astonishing that she's not faking this. And that, Lamm recognized amid Malik Massawi's ghostly eruption, is your attraction. Your misshaped animal magnetism, your degenerate chaos, invigorates this princess via her thirst for self-destruction. The reason you're here.

Again, Lamm tried to look away from the slain teenager's horrifying phantom. Ignore the bloodstains! Feel Kelly's tits, her fleshy outcrops swollen like the Hindenburg moments before disaster. Look at her white white teeth, spindly waxed arms, tanned concave stomach assured of skinniness by a daily half-hour's sit-ups (a disciplinary relic of the National Guard) *and* the bulimia. The slender exclamation point of waxed pink flesh just above her pussy; the things that teenage boys dream of!

'C-c-come on!' she stammered.

Why's it taking you so long? Don't I turn you on?

The problem: Lamm gazed not at the exquisite crimson gash below, at her velvety delectation exciting his reproductive urge, life and death incarnate. Instead he stared into Malik's writhing bleeding eyes, into the dead boy's shattered skull, his soul.

Ghost! Say something! Let me fuck her!

If you're the reaper bringing death, bring it!

But Malik Massawi didn't gesture nor speak. He stared at Lamm, the ghastly cascade of wriggling maggots, putrefied blood plasma, festering skin, bulbous pus slopping out his eyes, over his eyelashes, down his nose, cheeks, chin onto the bloodstained sheets. All over Kelly's thighs, her pussy and Lamm's abdomen, the ghost's excretory waterfall of decay, decortication, decomposition.

'*Do it!*'

But Lamm couldn't, not with her breasts painted sickening scarlet by the juices from his victim's skull.

'*Fuck me!*'

She stammered the magic words, arousing as anything Lamm ever saw in a men's magazine or imagined as a schoolboy. She must have snorted some great stuff earlier. Digging her fingernails into his arse, she forced him in so hard it seemed her midriff would collapse. Arching her pelvis, heels scraping the backs of his thighs. But Lamm couldn't look away from the boy's ghost.

'*Now!*'

Finally — as Malik's face erupted blood, maggots, pus, mucous, bile — the semen flowed too. Not from Lamm, however much he wanted to, *needed* to, but from the dead boy. A pearl trail of ejaculate squirted out of the ghost's eyes, out from his hollow pupils. Flowing down his cheeks onto Kelly's stomach, these white tears of semen stolen from Lamm's testicles.

'What's wrong?' Kelly pushed him away with her knees. 'You can't finish up?'

Her National Guard tone of voice. She was *ordering* her boy to ejaculate; they had been fucking for thirty-five minutes already. Maybe he's gay.

'Gimme a second,' Lamm whispered. He thrusted

quicker, smoother. Finally feeling the surge of the climax when, once again, he saw his victim's ghost. Malik Massawi sitting cross-legged on the pillow, his bashed-in forehead draining blood, piss, pus, cum, shit down onto the girl, cloaking her sensuality, concealing all that Lamm – all that anybody but a necrophiliac, coprophiliac madman! – would want from her angelic body. And amid the blood, his precious dollops of white! Kelly's chest glistened with the pearl drops of semen, thieved from Lamm's own vesicles by the teenage ghost.

Kelly sat up, sighing.

'Honey, that's enough or I'll need an ice pack.'

Lamm mumbled affirmatively. The sheets a drip-painting of blood, piss, pus, tears, shit, maggots and worms from Malik's freshly buried coffin. *There's a pattern in the bloodstains.* In the mosaic of vile fluids amassed upon the mattress, there was an image that Lamm recognized. Goya. *Saturn Eating His Son.* Painted in Malik Massawi's blood, Goya's deranged portrait of Saturn, the Roman sun-god, tearing the limbs off his own child. Eating his offspring, his future, in a cavernous hell.

Kelly pulled on her underwear. 'I'm taking a shower. Let's hope that next time you have a happy ending.'

She staggered onto the carpet, cupping her breasts. When Lamm looked back at the bed, the sheets were white as ever.

NINETEEN

Kelly's stepsister, Jacqueline LaRoy, worked in public relations. She too had escaped Washington, London being her sabbatical from a lobbying job at Covington & Burling, the powerful K Street law firm where her uncle Jim was a senior partner. She was a future White House press secretary, her mother reminded her, if she travelled in the right circles; those circles, tight as a hangman's noose, restricted to career sycophants or journalists who write the right things about the right people. Jacqueline didn't mind the work; preparing briefs, taking calls, meeting congressmen for lavish long lunches at Signatures, the Penn Quarter restaurant owned by the corrupt lobbyist Jack Abramoff before his downfall. She'd fly first class to hobnob with important clients like Chevron, Halliburton or Phillip Morris, and occasionally watch baseball games in a skybox with Republican fat cats. Not a lawyer – she majored in media communications at Penn State – and not quite a lobbyist, yet on account of her mother's second husband, she was invited to meet and greet the big players.

Talking was Jacqueline LaRoy's greatest attribute. Like her powerful stepfather, she was a cloistered thinker offering few new insights yet wielding an astonishing talent for bluster and hype. She'd cut her teeth at bullshit when she worked for an internet start-up in Fresno before the dotcom crash. The way she talked up that web firm with its tantalizing pay-offs, its impossible profit margins on poster graphs showing volcanic market capitalization! She did the work with such gusto and, it couldn't be ignored, flirtatiousness in a short skirt and pumps, that before it went belly-up and got sold to AT&T for peanuts, the business attracted millions in investment from two yoga-loving venture capitalists down in San Francisco.

But Jacqueline needed a rest. A rest from stalking the holidaying Bushes up at Kennebunkport, a rest from the Capitol catfights, from saying yes to fossilized Pentagon sleazeballs who, deep in the autumn of their virility, achieved a hard-on from contemplating bunker-busting bombs and her breasts. While Kelly tortured the cleaning staff at the Maryland National Guard, Jacqueline decamped to her stepdad's luxury London apartment. Conveniently abroad during the Abramoff scandal (her number was in his mobile phone), she couldn't take the journalists' calls. London was Jacqueline's recuperative break from the usual Washington chores: digging dirt on her stepfather's enemies, taking Big Oil execs for long lunches with the Secretary of the Interior, or organizing weekend hunting trips for Dick Cheney, Justice Scalia, her stepfather and other formaldehyde Republicans, watching the red-faced warmongers breaking grouse necks as they fumed about the Syrians, the Iranians, missile defence shields, same-sex spouses . . .

It wasn't that Jacqueline and her stepfather didn't agree about the defence budget, tax cuts for the rich, gay marriage, family values, the whole conservative hootenanny; but she was *sick* of agreeing. Sick of the daily rhetorical engagement about healthcare, Saudi oil, Guantanamo, unilateralism, the liberal bias in the *Post* or her clients' interviews on Fox News. Sick of the incessant incendiary blabber that stole her weekends, weeknights and dreams. Worse, Jacqueline's job extinguished her desire for a man. Within her Beltway circles, the guys were stiffs, Phi Beta Kappa big mouths more interested in lunch with Bill O'Reilly than a Brazilian model on all fours. Clever young conservatives, professed Baptists or Likudnik Jews, these All-American men drove Jacqueline LaRoy *and* Kelly Wesson nuts. One of the few things the stepsisters agreed upon.

In London, Jacqueline was a strategic director at Green & Dwyer, a high-end PR firm in Greek Street. There she captivated the clients with a sultry purr uncannily like her stepsister's. Jacqueline extolled the TV spots, magazine covers, newspaper profiles, product endorsements . . . all the promotional gems obtainable if only you jump through the flaming shit-drenched hoops. Not biologically a Wesson, but, more than his real daughter, Jacqueline possessed her stepfather's knack for advertising, for the essential effluent of capitalism sludging through the newsstands, the airwaves, the city streets until the whole world's its neon sewer. Makes such a stink we don't notice the smell.

The afternoon Kelly invited home the boy from the barbeque, Jacqueline was away on a junket to Paris. Her hectic week at the spring fashion parades, amid the seasonal maelstrom of expressionless teenage models, hyperventilating designers, B-list film stars, professional hangers-on and everywhere Columbia's most prominent cash crop. Jacqueline's assignment: to build recognition for Dior's new handbag, a crocodile skin lesson in how to throw two-and-a-half-thousand quid down the toilet. She faced the usual conundrums. Who should get the gilded handbags for free? Where's the blonde daughter of Mick or Keef who's in the magazines this week?

The narcissistic inanity of the wealthy quarry never troubled Jacqueline, nor her rival PR queens, expert at blowdrys and blowjobs, for whom life resembled a DVD; you fast-forward through the boring bits. And the party boys! Those chiselled *ubermenschen*, the longhaired Aryan stags in Slimane leathers who would have sent Leni Riefenstahl and Joseph Goebells gaga, for whom catastrophe isn't Stalingrad but a botched photo shoot or an uneven tan. Jacqueline enjoyed the London–Paris–NYC axis of drunk fucks, pricey powders, secret nightclubs; of cynical post-everything doubletalk, of everyone being an aspiring fashion designer, of dance floors with strobe lights simulating the amphetamine pulse of a racehorse. A peerlessly vacuous world of beauties transfixed by beauty, blind to the written word, unable to read between the lines unless they're snorted. Embrace the bullshit! Eat it, drink it, swim in it, love it! Jacqueline hadn't previously realized that so many words can say so little.

But after eighteen months on the job, Jacqueline yearned for Washington. She wanted to again work with her stepdad's grizzled Reaganites who could teach her more than make-up tips and bedroom technique, for whom the whole world isn't a designer boutique in Mayfair but a precious American oyster being hacked open by Al-Qaeda and the Chinese. She wanted to learn. So the morning of Chanel's spring parade on the Champs Élysées, Jacqueline LaRoy made up her mind. She gave her VIP laminate to a teenage girl gazing longingly at the red carpet, took the

3 p.m. Eurostar and arrived at Victoria Station a day early. The Saturday her stepfather was to land in London en route from the World Economic Forum in Switzerland.

'You're back *now*?' Kelly stammered into the phone. 'You said he was visiting Monday!'

Kelly lay a fingertip upon Lamm's lips; *be silent on pain of death*. Painfully, Kelly gazed at the living room, apprehending the challenge ahead. Château d'Yquem spilt on the rug, takeaway cartons strewn about, charcoal dust in the carpet, powder traces on the coffee table, Marlboro butts clogging the sink, a fugitive homeless Jew on the sofa.

'Fine, we'll do dinner.' Kelly slammed down the phone. 'We have to clean up! *Now!*'

Scrubbing wine stains, packing the dishwasher, scouring the sink, replenishing Jacqueline's Valium with identical-looking aspirins and, hardest of all, checking there wasn't a grain of contraband powder left on the coffee table or the nightstand; it took longer than expected. Seventeen minutes later, they were cleaning when the door bell beeped. Kelly scrambled for the remote control, flicking to the surveillance channel on TV. Onscreen was a middle-aged man in a suit, standing in the lobby.

'I *cannot* fucking believe this! He's here!'

Kelly rushed Lamm into the master bedroom. She opened the walk-in wardrobe.

'Hide on top. He *will* check everywhere.'

'It won't hold my weight.'

'Ha! His rope will. Get up there!'

She darted out to the corridor, glancing up at the closet.

Their eyes met. For the first time since their confrontation

183

in the park, they stared relentlessly into each other's faces. Of course they had watched each other in bed, confirming the mutual release. But now, their gaze was undistracted by the imminent act. What Lamm and Kelly saw was immense vulnerability, the embryonic connection of two damaged vessels mending themselves with a single gauze. They saw their loneliness obliterated *and* emphasized in the hours they spent together, enraptured by the infatuated other. She the lifeboat, he the squall. In Lamm's unblinking gaze, he said: even if I had never encountered that Pakistani mugger at 4 a.m. in a Camden street, you would be my salvation. In your generosity, your appetites, your wonderful, horrible history, in your bewildering desire, I'm a success and not fleeing a life that was already spent before that bottle struck the boy's skull. You are a blessing for a neglectful Jew who forgets the *mitzvoth* and only visits a synagogue because he killed someone. After humiliation, exile, catastrophe, after the deathly embrace of New York's river, I deserve you. Not for my virtues but my sins, because suffering must end. With darkness comes light.

She saw it. The premature outline of love that coalesced immeasurably into the axis of their gaze. Their unwavering stare of about eleven seconds, conveying her ascension, her redemption in assisting this statuesque stranger whose secret, apart from his expert caress, drew her further in. Damaged by some event of unimagined consequences, battered by a ghastly truth – she saw the evidence in Lamm's failure to ejaculate while he watched his victim's ghost – that was fascinating and frightening. Fascinating *because* it was frightening. In their exchange of words, opinions, interests – everything but the concealed facts of Lamm's crime and Kelly's sadistic rebirth in the National

Guard – their relationship was effortless, unforced. Their bond of choosing life amidst suicide and not understanding why, of forever betraying their family's expectations, of being dumbstruck by the animal catharsis of their dim hot hours in that four-poster bed – *that*, in their rebirth, in the shrapnel of their trauma, in their primitive love incinerating loneliness – that is what kept Lamm and Kelly staring at each other for eleven seconds while the doorbell rang out.

This wardrobe was bigger than your average African's shack. Lamm closed the door, then scrambled onto the top shelf packed with pillowslips, sheets, blankets, a green National Guard sleeping bag. He pulled himself into the corner; the support beams felt strong enough. Now you'll hear – see? – Dick Wesson in the flesh. The Minotaur. If that bastard discovers you, he'll unleash the CIA. They'll fly you to Cairo where an interrogator drowns you until you confess that Bin Laden's your ping-pong partner. Lamm lay tight against the wall, concealed behind laundered blankets the way his cat Misty used to sleep among his mother's scarves.

What's your life compared to this? She's got three Tuscan lambswool blankets wrapped in plastic. Never been used; still got the price tag from Harrods. One hundred and fifteen pounds each. Your father would fly these rugs from a flagpole.

Voices reverberated down the corridor.

Don't let the blankets fall.

Don't move.

Don't breathe.

Lamm gasped.

Touching his right thigh, there was a handgun wrapped in the mohair rug.

A .45. Silver, cold to the touch. Lamm knew nothing about guns, but noticed that the safety was on. Surely, she doesn't know that it's here. Senator Wesson, the chairman of the Senate Armed Services Committee, can't be so stupid as to assign a loaded weapon to a girl so tempestuous, tumultuous, drug-addled as his daughter. No, it's here for his own protection. The Minotaur applies the Second Amendment to whichever country he's in.

Never had Lamm been closer to a pistol than the nearest policeman's holster. The diaspora Jews don't keep guns; they've got lawyers. He gripped the stock and unclicked the clip. The cartridges slipped onto the blanket. Lamm crammed the pistol and ammunition into his jeans pocket.

'So how are my favourite girls in London?'

Snatches of conversation resonating through the plaster walls. Five million pounds and it's not solid brick.

'How did the wine get on the rug?'

A woman's voice; must be the half-sister.

'Steve, how about a cold drink?'

'Thank you, Miss. I'd appreciate that.'

Steve's was a dull, deep voice, emotionless in the military sense. Must be the bodyguard.

The voices faded; they're out on the balcony. Lamm waited twenty-three minutes by his watch, sweating into the blankets. Finally the talking got louder.

'Gimme the number for The Ivy in Covent Garden . . . Thank you.'

The senator speaking into his mobile phone.

'Table for three . . . eight o'clock. That's right . . .'

Kelly's voice echoed down the marble corridor.

'I'll get my coat.'

Bright light flooded the master bedroom. Lamm piled

the blankets over his torso. Through the venetian door, he glimpsed Jacqueline. Different than what he'd imagined, so unlike her stepsister. A tall big-boned brunette in stilettos, a skirt to the knees, a white shirt. The Amazonian build of a women's basketball pro, and on her chin a mole discernable from Lamm's vantage.

The senator walked in, clasping Kelly's shoulders. Immediately Lamm felt this gargantuan presence unleashed from the CSPAN screen. The Minotaur's brute aura, all bluster, rambunctiousness, unhindered confidence. A living incarnation of the Bill of Rights, starkly there in the Reaganesque way he talked, in his Washington-via-Texas drawl dripping in the unwavering numbskull doggedness that politicians call resolve. No wonder he'd come so far, finally a credible contender for the Republican presidential nomination. Sixty years old, silver-haired, with a hook-nosed profile that would've landed him a role as the villain in a Sergio Leone spaghetti western. One of the Minotaur's harshest critics, Senator Max Cleland of Georgia (who lost two legs and an arm in Vietnam), once joked on *Meet the Press* that Dick Wesson was the other most disabled member of the Senate, owing to his leg injury inflicted in 2003 by an insolent riding colt (long since dog food) down at George W's ranch at Crawford. Despite his knee reconstruction, Dick Wesson marched into the master bedroom like Napoleon victorious at the Battle of Austerlitz.

Look at the father of the girl you're screwing. Look at what's gotten him where he is.

It's the razor contrast of his sky-blue eyes to the leathery fatherly brow; the avuncular grey tips of his eyebrows, the drill sergeant's voice so unrepentantly decisive. A man accustomed to getting his way, whether it's creationism in

Kansas schools, tariffs against Chinese grain imports, federal legislation against gay marriage or tonight's short-notice table for three at The Ivy in Covent Garden.

The Minotaur inspected the master bedroom.

'This place looks rough. The guests won't come in here.'

The guests. *That's* the reason for the deli in the refrigerator! Must be a dinner party here tomorrow night. Tony and Cherie, Messrs Branson, Lord Levy and Al Fayed.

The senator glanced at the crumpled bedspread, the crooked pillows.

'In the National Guard, they never taught you how to make a bed?'

'Make the fucking bed yourself.'

A numb silence. The Minotaur laughed.

If I didn't need you, his chuckle told Kelly, *I'd throw you out onto the fucking street.*

Light exploded into the wardrobe. *Don't breathe!* Three feet away, the Minotaur. His helmet of gunmetal-grey hair, his liver-spotted forehead, craggy cheekbones, capped teeth, pink bull's neck, an American flag pinned to his herringbone sports jacket's lapel.

'No boys hiding in the closet! Oh, my visit was in vain!'

Through a sliver in the blankets, Lamm watched Kelly crack a smile.

You're not just her new boy. You're a game to her.

The Minotaur strolled into the corridor.

'Steve, we're going! Call the maître d', tell him we don't sit near the window.'

Kelly stepped into the closet, grabbed a Jil Sander coat and winked at the top shelf. Gone without a word. The front door slammed shut. Lamm heard the car starting outside, a fearsome guttural rumble. Probably an armoured limo from the US embassy.

He waited fifteen minutes. Hearing the blood in his ear canal and the faint hum of Oxford Street traffic, Lamm decided to climb down. Yet beyond the usual anxiety pervading his universe like the ether, something was wrong. He couldn't move one foot. Buried beneath blankets, Lamm's right leg had gone to sleep. He rubbed his numb calf, trying to get the circulation back, then fully stretched the leg. The shelf's load of blankets crashed down, scattering Kelly's Italian heels.

'*Arghhhhh!*' Lamm bit his tongue to stop himself cursing.

Squeezing, rubbing, the sensation returned to Lamm's tingling prosthesis. Gingerly, he crept down to clean up the mess.

You have a gun. Your last resort via ultimatum, self-defence or suicide. Compulsively, Lamm checked it was unloaded. Go hide it in the barbeque! He tried to re-stack the blankets, but again they tumbled down. A closet the size of a Cadillac, still the rugs don't fit! He pulled them out for another try, and noticed something wedged way back on the shelf. Another gun? Lamm climbed up and yanked the mystery object from beneath the pillowcases. An old shoebox. There's something inside, too light to be shoes.

This must belong to the senator. It's CIA secrets on microfilm? The identity of whoever really bombed Pan Am 103, sold Saddam the phantom WMDs, or killed JFK, Vince Foster, Dr David Kelly, Yasser Arafat? Hopefully it's cash, enough to buy a passport from Zayed the barber.

Lamm pulled off the lid. A shoebox of family photos. Old school snaps of Kelly and her brother, and a few yellowing portraits of the senator in his Skull & Bones days. Newspaper clippings of Wesson's election victories, a signed Christmas card from Nancy Reagan, and holiday photos – Hawaii when Kelly was fifteen, and Puerto Rico nine years ago – showing a happy family on the beach. A lie as it often is: Kelly's dull eyes and flatlined lips expressed how she hated the sand, the sun, the sagging swimsuits. Nothing extraordinary here; just memories amassed in a dusty shoebox that will keep its shape longer than your neurons destined to be mush. No photo more provocative than the holiday photos that millions of Americans keep in their shoeboxes.

Except for one.

Deep in the box, way down the bottom, a photograph stole Lamm's attention. It featured a blonde man, perhaps twenty-five years old, sitting on a bar stool. A tight white singlet accentuated his muscular arms, rock-hard abdominals, toned hairless chest. Up top, buzz-cut fair hair framed his exquisitely proportioned face; sharp chin, pursed full lips, prominent cheekbones, narrow aqua-blue eyes. The captivating bone structure of the alpha-male; strikingly symmetrical, unmistakably masculine. Look at what testosterone's done to this beautiful boy! One hand dangled a cigarette, the other touched the belt buckle of his tight blue jeans. He stared into the lens. Fearless, feisty, fuck-ready, like the angelic young Brando in *The Wild One* asking, 'Whattya got?'

On the back of the photo, a name and number in red ink.

BOBBY. 0207 968 965. CALL AFTER NINE

Lamm buried the photo in the shoebox, but couldn't resist another peek. One of Kelly's toyboys? Had to be, but couldn't be. Despite the sky-high cheekbones, the washboard stomach, Lamm knew that beautiful Bobby wasn't Kelly's type. He looked too perfect, too calculatingly submissive. Too damn easy. Whereas Kelly – ceaselessly drunk on her lifeblood of transgression, dissent, disorder – always thirsted for the challenge. To fuck the guy she shouldn't; that's why *you're* here. No, she wouldn't like the blonde figurine in this photograph. The type of Aryan idol – a pure pink sculpture of muscle, sweat, skin – who's been the perennial pin-up for the Wehrmacht, the Red Army, the US Marines, the Ivy League. Kelly, Lamm was sure, hated clean-cut specimens like Bobby, the type of boy the Minotaur would invite home for a beer out on the back porch.

Nevertheless, the phone number in red looked written especially for someone.

They might return any moment. What if the senator or the big-boned stepsister had forgotten their wallet or keys? Yet, exhilarated by his near-miss in the closet, by evading the conservative warhorse whose insatiable daughter he was screwing, Lamm felt alive! More alive than he'd felt since . . . the night he drowned in the East River? The morning he awoke from his coma at New York Hospital? Haunted, hungry Lamm! He didn't want prison, or a lynching from Malik's vigilante avengers, or to atone for his crime or else suffer guilt, madness, damnation. Didn't want *not* to live, to rot undiscovered beneath a Hyde Park barbeque, to envisage Malik's eyes squirting semen stolen from his own vesicles, to see his eternal sweetheart's ghost in a foreign synagogue. He wanted to go home! To evade the police, the tabloids, the vengeful gangs, to return to Melbourne's Jewish enclave where he would hug his late grandmother and eat her homemade *kugelhopf*. You are not a lemming! You will not wait in this wardrobe until J Edgar Hoover returns from dinner!

In two minutes Lamm returned the shoebox to its hiding spot, stuffed the blankets onto the shelf, then fled down the stairs. He ran into Hyde Park, another skinny young man on his evening jog. Go hide the gun beneath the barbeque.

TWENTY

Lamm sat on the stone rim of a birdbath embossed with dried chewing gum. He gazed east through the trees. There, over the dim shag of willows' fringes, glowed the clock above Queensway Tube station. 1.26 a.m. They would have returned home three hours ago. Kelly collapsing on her bed to watch MTV all night and snort crushed tablets of Seroquel, an anti-psychotic that doubles as a sedative; Jacqueline opening her laptop to check the voluminous influx of emails, press releases, party invites, friend requests; the senator relaxing on the marble toilet, reading the *Wall Street Journal* as he bid farewell to the £65 lobster.

Tomorrow is Monday, the first day of your second week of *this*. The beginning of the end. The banks will be open, so ask Kelly for the money. Five thousand pounds for a fake passport. Tell her that you're a drug mule on the run, she can relate to that. Perhaps her father's visit has sufficiently perturbed her that she'll do something so irrational? If she won't lend you the cash, will she reject you for asking? In families like hers, the financial sixth sense is indestructible.

Of course, Lamm knew the exaggerated reports of Hyde Park after dark. A no-man's land of foxes, squirrels, rats clawing the undergrowth; of muggers, homeless bums, gay men cruising the late-night beats. According to the mums and dads of wealthy West London, nocturnal Hyde Park is the Brazilian favela meets Caligula's rape chamber. Yet who in this park has committed a worse crime than yours? *You're the terror.*

Near the grey shimmering fountain, three cigarettes pinpricked the dim. A trio of closet queens, hooking up away from prying eyes. They're Hyde Park's husbands satisfying their mundane secret. The sky unusually clear tonight, its silvery pinhole sequins multiplied a thousandfold. Unimaginably far from your mess, the stars ancient, cold, intractable.

That moment, dazzled by the constellations unusually bright for central London, Lamm recalled – *saw* – his eighth-grade school excursion to the McKay Planetarium at the old Melbourne Museum in Swanston Street. The afternoon that Brian Zwinger, a school parent, professor of astrophysics at Monash University and Mr Lewski's squash partner, engrossed eighty-four students with comets, asteroids, planetary nebulae, turbulent quasars eating stars, white dwarfs, red giants, pulsars signalling for aeons like perpetual interstellar lighthouses, black holes devouring light and time itself, the big bang and the beginning and end of it all (which might really be the same event).

The eighth graders stuck their hands up, asking the distinguished professor about *ET*, *Close Encounters of the Third Kind*, *Star Trek* or the alleged UFO crash at Roswell in New Mexico. With his percipient thirst for knowledge (frustrated by the dull conversations he endured with gorilla training partners on the tennis court), Lamm was especially fascinated by Professor Zwinger's description of how the elements came to exist. The ferocious, elegant process: the elements' evolution in stellar furnaces, expulsion as stardust, incorporation into the lumps of rock that formed planets, where finally they became the air, minerals and water that sustains life. *Everything* on Earth, the professor announced – the pink soft stuff of your brain, the green trees, black soil, purple clouds, cantaloupes, fruitbats, surgeons' scalpels, stealth bombers, Siberian tigers, undiscovered diamonds, the sky, the air, this page and this hyphen, everything, anything! – was cooked up in an exploding star. Professor Zwinger liked to speak with his hands, a charming incarnation of the stereotypical science boffin in his Georges corduroy jacket, short clipped beard and thick glasses (he was shortsighted from years of staring into the 2.0 m telescope atop Siding Spring Mountain near Coonabarabran).

'See, kids? We're *stardust*! We're made from elements that were manufactured in stars! We're mostly carbon that's billions of years old, cooked up from hydrogen compressed inside a supernova that exploded with the energy of a trillion H-bombs!'

Professor Zwinger clicked onto the next slide: a diagrammatic sketch of hydrogen fused in a star's core.

'Over *billions* of years, the cosmic dust from exploded supernovas sticks together through gravity. Gradually, the dust clumps into new stars, asteroids and planets, including our home three rocks along from the sun. Any questions?'

Another student – the third in thirty minutes – asked if UFOs would attack New York City like in the movies. But Lamm was engrossed by his own hands. Stardust, eh? Your skin, fingerprints, notches, cracks, scratches. The five-fingered creations of flesh that you use for eating, picking things up, playing tennis, writing with a pen, jacking off. It's all exploded stardust, besmirched! *You're made from disaster, you make disaster.*

Zwinger requested a volunteer from the audience. The lucky kid would win a Melbourne Planetarium badge-pin. Amid the frantic chorus of *me! me! me!*, he selected an uninterested girl adjusting her knee socks in the front row Reluctantly she answered her name: Rachel Samuels.

Not that her introduction was required. To the boys in Rachel's class, she was the conversation topic, shared obsession, unobtainable quarry. Onstage, she showcased that bewitching nervous smile – two slightly crooked bottom teeth accentuating her face's symmetrical perfection – and her crowd-pleasing precocious breasts. She followed Professor Zwinger's instructions, at the right moment touching the gleaming spherical electrode of his mini Van Der Graaf generator. The younger kids roared as static electricity spiked Rachel's hair up like a spaghettified cauliflower, while the eighth-grade boys were hypnotized by her tight school dress, her nubile nippled marvels that induced many a schoolboy's first experiments with Vaseline behind the locked bathroom door. Those breasts, her glassy aquamarine eyes, the superior unperturbed look she shot at the leering classmates. The haunting wet dream of Lamm's adolescence, Rachel Samuels too was stardust.

How defiantly she glared at the stiff salivating boys! More desirable for her resolve *not* to be embarrassed. Then the astonishing moment: from the planetarium's stage, Rachel Samuels stared at the skinny tennis champ in the second row. Those incredible five seconds returning to Lamm as he wondered – hoped! – whether her ghost would again haunt him tonight.

That school excursion when they first locked glances.

Rachel was fourteen years old, yet already accomplished at wordlessly telling a hopeless voyeur what he needed to know. She spelt *'you're a pervert'* with the tilt of an eyebrow. Who would've thought eyebrows grew like hers? So thin, dark, emphatic! Despite the apocalyptic realization that Rachel had identified his infatuation – this was, after all, his most nerve-wracking moment since his bar mitzvah speech a month earlier – Lamm maintained his gaze as she returned to her seat on the planetarium floor.

Rachel turned around and stared at Max Lamm. Her earthquake. A strange soft look – *I know you're watching me, I know why and I like it* – that never wavered, never stopped; not two days later when they kissed during the intermission of *Fiddler on the Roof*, not when she went to London that summer and sent him four gigantic words in pink marker on a postcard of Trafalgar Square: LONDON SUCKS. LOVE RACHEL. Her expectant, excoriating glance invaded Lamm's thirteenth year, invaded his dreams until he awoke in sodden boxer shorts. Every year, every moment since, their afternoon at the old Melbourne Museum had strengthened in his memory; all the exquisite excruciating details. Her stare that promised something astonishing for a thirteen-year-old boy, something revelatory and truthful, until the evening of 21 December, 1988, when she was blown out of a bombed Pan Am airliner into the dark Scottish sky. Rachel too was ageless, indestructible stardust, and she was gone.

Lamm checked his watch: 2.16 a.m. For nearly an hour, he had been dozing in this empty birdbath. Comfortably collapsed against the granite backboard carved with a red-breasted robin blind from cataracts of hard bubblegum upon either eye. Icy dew glazed his forehead, his shoulders ached, his hunger surged.

Lamm hurried to buy food. To the convenience store on Great Cumberland Place, for another microwaved pumpkin pie.

About a hundred metres off the path, a gardener's shed stood beneath a weeping willow. Lamm stopped, still. An unnervingly familiar sound emanated from that padlocked windowless cube of painted chipboard and corrugated perspex. The hair on his arms, the noradrenalin in his blood-stream surged upwards as Lamm's sympathetic nervous system – the fight or flight response – sprang into gear.

It was the sound of somebody coughing. Not just *any* cough; Lamm didn't presume this was a homeless bum with a chest infection. This wheezing, overdone cough sounded uncannily familiar. Intoned not only by phlegm, but a sharp American – Texan? – take on the '*arghhhh*' sound rolled in the larynx. An exaggerated half-spoken cough, expelled the way John Wayne elongated his vowels to pronounce 'parachute' as '*per-aaah-shoot*'. Creeping closer, Lamm suspected that he had heard this cough very recently.

You have!

It was a cough due to a chest complaint, Lamm remembered from what he'd overheard that afternoon, which had persisted despite the dry microclimate up at Davos in the Swiss Alps, venue of last week's World Economic Forum.

In the lavender bushes, the noise got louder.

'*Arghhhh . . . ahhhh . . . ahhhh . . .*'

Something else in that cough too; not just obstruction of the airways or saturation of the alveoli. A moan, a sigh, a pleasurable pant. Lamm recognized it intimately: catharsis! An asthmatic crescendo of ecstasy!

Gingerly, Lamm crept around the gardener's shed. Treading on a brittle twig, he froze at its crack. But whoever was moaning, they weren't listening for interlopers. The muffled groans, interspersed with coughing, got louder as Lamm discovered the source.

In the grey moonlight, two men heaved behind the shed. A tall dark-haired guy, trousers around his ankles, knelt in the damp leaves. Breathing through his nose, his lips were enwrapped around somebody's dick. Forwards, back, forwards the man's head rocked.

Lamm knelt too. Carefully he edged forward, through the scrub, until there was no mistaking the identity of the recipient. Lamm watched the Minotaur groan towards his climax. After what seemed like aeons more sucking, gingerly the senator pushed the mystery man away from his groin.

'Okay, Larry. It's your turn now.'

Sworn enemy of the Beijing sweatshop imperialists! Steadfast guardian of star-spangled military dominance! Champion of pre-emptive regime change for the Islamofascist kleptocracies! Obstinate foe of Saddam, Kim Jong Il, the Ayatollahs and Ted Kennedy, unofficial oil baron, sitting chairman of the Senate Armed Services Committee, this year's after-dinner speaker at the NRA's Washington banquet. The silver-haired mentor to Oliver North, a riding partner to Reagan in his later years, the Senate representative most likely to eulogize Dr Kissinger when that leather-skinned warhorse goes to the great US embassy in the sky. Senator Richard Davis Wesson, a credible contender for the Republican presidential nomination, knelt in the leaves beneath a tall, uncircumcised, fortysomething man named Larry.

What, Lamm wondered, was Wesson thinking about *now*? Going down on Larry, did the senator imagine beefy shirtless Marines, phallic nuclear silos, erect uncircumcised missiles, cigar-shaped daisy cutters taking out the Iranian nukes and a few villages too, all to help the old hawk blow his load? The senator who, a fortnight earlier, had eloquently argued on *Meet The Press* that gay marriage was an affront to the founding fathers; who was a steadfast opponent of same-sex unions when the issue drove a wedge through the '04 election; who stood shoulder-to-shoulder with Pat Robertson and Jerry Falwell in Washington; who refused to meet the gay Log Cabin Republicans for fear of alienating Focus on the Family; who publicly lambasted David Geffen, Elton John, Jann Wenner and the other powerful gay advocates; who, every chance he got, denounced the sacrilege of two men marrying, was, in front of Lamm, sucking on Larry's dick with stamina, relish, expertise. Of course, the photograph of Bobby! The chiselled blonde gigolo, the phone number in red ink, hidden inside a shoebox in the wardrobe. Probably one of many.

And surely the senator isn't the only one. Must be other covert gays at Capitol Hill and the Pentagon, just as there are gay cowboys, gay navy SEALS, gay quarterbacks. But the potential of what he was witnessing, the beneficial volcano that it could unleash, didn't occur to Lamm until Larry was about to blow.

A way out!

Lamm's father appeared, floating above the dewy lavender bushes. Wearing his favourite Reebok tracksuit, wielding a racquet. The fire of this remarkable opportunity burning in his ghostly eyes. Mel Lamm's deep spectral voice was really many voices, combining the intonation of his son, of Mr Lewski, of Lamm's grandparents, school friends, doubles partners, teachers, coaches, neighbours . . . of everybody the young fugitive had ever met! The gestalt supernatural voice of Max Lamm's everything and nothing, of his past stripped naked and future unknown. What his father's ghost – hallucination? – suggested was what Lamm knew, clear as the moonlight.

'*Max, here's your chance! Blackmail the rich bastard!*'

The Minotaur would dig deep to stop Barbara Walters from frowning at his oral adventures. Enough for a fake passport and an extra few million too. Lamm crept from the bushes. Your camera phone won't work; the battery is empty. But at the convenience store on Great Cumberland Place, atop the counter next to the cigarette lighters and phone cards, there is, you will recall, a rack of Kodak disposable cameras on sale for £7 each.

Four minutes later, after the fastest, darkest sprint of his life, Lamm scaled the wrought-iron fence by Marble Arch, ran to the 24-7 store and purchased a camera. How much would the tabloids cough up if Wesson didn't? Unscrupulous, of course. A vicious, unethical thing to do. But hasn't the Minotaur's CIA done worse? Didn't the spooks plot to kill Castro, Allende, Trujillo and the other Latin leftists? Didn't they conjure Saddam's WMDs to justify their phony war?

Over the fence, through the carnation bed, down the embankment, onto the path, past the fountains, right at the weeping willow, into the lavender bushes. Where's the gardener's shed? Lamm backtracked, listening. There, the soft ecstatic groans! Creeping through the chrysanthemums, he made certain the camera's flash was turned on.

Snap!

In the half-second of illumination, Lamm recognized the craggy Mount Rushmore jaw, the Caesarean nose, the silver hair starkly framed by the shed wall on one side, Larry's hairy thighs on the other. The libidinous diorama of two trouserless men, frozen in the flash of Lamm's doomsday flare. Immediately, he wound the film and snapped again. The senator turned, his lips embracing Larry's scrotum, as the mystery photographer escaped into the bushes. A scream curled from Wesson's lips: pure horror.

How many times, Lamm wondered as he tore through the undergrowth, has Wesson recklessly fucked at 2 a.m. in a park, or in a hotel room or a motel cabin, and never been caught? Nevertheless, Washington's most powerful men are capable of decisions that would make a toddler blush.

Wet branches whipping his face, Lamm fled through the chrysanthemum bed. The Minotaur's bodyguards will be here soon! Go underground, hide the camera! He rounded a bend, looking for the deformed rubbish bin that signposted the path to the barbeque.

There it is!

As Lamm ran onto the brambled path, a black mass of desperation sprang from the trees, tackling him to the ground. The silver hair, the owl's eyebrows, the unbuttoned fly.

'Give me the camera!'

A sticky fist struck Lamm's face; blood sputtered out his left nostril. But the Pentagon hawk wasn't as strong as he sounded, softened by thirty years of long limos and longer lunches. No match for a twenty-eight-year-old vagrant who, despite his encroaching madness and unwashed decrepitude, still retained the explosive guile of a tennis ace. Again, Lamm was in gym class at high school, wrestling Marty Weinberg in a half-circle of classmates who had bet five dollars on the winner. He remembered an old trick; the right-handed half-nelson. Lamm slammed his torso onto the grass, gripping the senator's neck so hard that surely his fingernails drew blood, and kicked the hyperventilating warhorse backwards into a juniper bush. Free, the fugitive sprang into the trees.

'*Stop or I'll shoot your fucking head off.*'

In the magisterial American rumble that transfixed his thirty-five thousand dollar-a-speech audiences, the Senator howled into the blackness.

But why hasn't he shot you already? Because his .45 is hidden beneath your barbeque. The senator doesn't bring his bodyguards on this type of excursion.

Lamm scrambled into the hole. He faintly heard the senator yelling into his mobile phone.

'Steve, I'm in Hyde Park! I've been attacked!'

TWENTY-ONE

Underground, Lamm lay in the charcoal dust. Waiting. Listening. Feeling the cold dangerous bulge of the camera in his right trouser pocket. Within minutes, he heard voices nearby. The faint crackle of a radio, the type used by secret service agents with a wire in their ear.

They're looking for you.

Those bodyguards might have walked right past the barbeque. For nine hours, Lamm remained underground; falling asleep, waking, sleeping, pissing into an orange juice bottle. What excuse had the senator cooked up? That he was mugged during a midnight walk? He wouldn't tell the police; they're too indiscrete. Only Wesson's bodyguards are on your trail, searching for the paparazzi pauper who might undo a potential president.

Dusk. Reddish light drained through wormlike cracks in the barbeque's limestone walls. Finally, hearing only the murmur of traffic bending around Marble Arch, Lamm pushed the grate ajar. He inhaled a deep dustless breath, stretching his limbs. Hooded, Lamm waited until Bayswater Road was clear both ways. He jumped the fence and hurried down Queensway, past the shawarma stands, pirate DVD merchants and adolescent hoodlums amassed outside the subterranean bowling alley, into a shopping emporium where, he remembered, there was a one-hour-photo stall in the same arcade as Zayed the barber.

Quickly, Lamm used up the twenty-one shots remaining on the camera's film. He photographed the arcade's ceiling; its mouldy patches, cobwebs, old whirring fans that might any moment fly off and decapitate an unsuspecting shopper as they haggled the price of a baklava. He photographed the CCTV cameras photographing everybody, the masonite floor minutely cracked like a dry riverbed, the shops full of plastic from China – £5 clock radios, £10 CD players, kitchen appliances stamped with imitation insignias (Sonny, Palsonic, Sonyo) – hawked by a bearded vendor wearing a *keffiyeh* scarf and a white linen robe who, were it not for his mobile phone with a wireless earpiece, could have been a nineteenth-century Bedouin tribesman magically dumped in West London's oasis of crap.

Further in, Persian women in hijabs bought pistachios, dried figs, treacly yellow hummus, green peppers a forearm's length long. Iraqi men sold second-hand laptops, mostly to Indian students recently arrived in London to study software engineering and work at convenience stores. An internet café too, crowded by precociously moustached teenage boys looking at porn websites and gossiping online in Arabic and Farsi. These kids, taking a breather from skulking outside the bowling alley, wore plastic diamond studs in their left ears, imitation gold bracelets, and usually baggy windbreakers printed with some logo incorporating the US flag, presumably to the chagrin of the Islamists who, the *Daily Mail* reported, came to Queensway Road from the Finsbury Park mosque to hand out flyers espousing the heavenly merits of martyrdom.

Lamm found the one-hour-photo shop. At the counter

was a grey Iranian woman wearing tortoiseshell reading glasses and engrossed in a Farsi newspaper. The front page featured a colour photograph of President Ahmadinejad in his safari suit, standing at a flowery podium, his outstretched right hand seemingly stroking the nose of the Ayatollah in a giant hagiographic portrait onstage. This lady won't closely examine your photos. And if she does, so what? Is it illegal to photograph a prominent man sucking off a stranger in a public park?

For an hour, Lamm waited in the lounge at the rear of the arcade. For £3 he ate a tangy mash of yellow beans and couscous, and watched Al Jazeera on a flickering TV perched on a metal frame above a faded poster of Mount Damavand, the highest peak in Iran. The regular customers were men in sandals, beige slacks and open pastel shirts showcasing their stupefyingly hirsute chests. Their businesses, Lamm guessed, being imports back to Beirut, Damascus, Tehran, Baghdad. Speaking what sounded like ten different Arabian dialects, the men argued, laughed, ate pita with baba ghanoush, drank pungent black tea made from a Middle Eastern dried shrub, and played cards with a deck Lamm didn't recognize. They rarely glanced at the TV blaring in Arabic; the mundane news of car bombs, dead babies in Basra, a firestorm in Fallujah or the invader's latest proclamation of victory as another five thousand high school drop-outs from the foreclosing farmland of Kansas or the ghettos of Detroit surged into the Sunni Triangle, motivated not by patriotic bloodlust but by the military pension, subsidized healthcare and college tuition guaranteed by the Pentagon if they get back home alive.

The Lebanese, Syrian, Iranian, Iraqi businessmen only looked at the TV, finally distracted from their pungent tea and sweet halva, when the anchorman – a moustached square-jawed specimen of Arabian masculinity who would have made Lawrence of Arabia hard beneath his cream robes – reported the race riots in Bethnal Green. As the TV showed the grieving family of the Pakistani boy whose death had precipitated London's hot-headed disaster, the men in the coffee lounge cursed at the screen. Lamm watched too, noticing the hard, fresh creases in the face of Malik Massawi's weeping mother, the teary shellshock in the eyes of Malik Massawi's sisters and the black resignation sunk deeply into the stare of Malik Massawi's father, Nawaz, who glared at the TV cameras as he left the Brick Lane mosque the morning of his son's funeral. Nawaz Massawi who had escaped the death stalking every cranny of Kandahar, who had built a steady income as a house-painter by day and taxi driver by night, who had embraced the opportunities of the colonial motherland and raised a healthy young family until disorder met his eldest son at 4 a.m. in a deserted Camden street.

The hour had passed. Lamm left his plate empty, returned to the photo stall, paid the fee, then hurried to a public toilet by the entrance to Kensington Gardens. In a cubicle, he shuffled through the photos. Mostly they showed the arcade's scratched floor, fluorescent lights, bored shopkeepers looking out for shoplifters with one eye and at the Arabic newspaper with the other. Then the prize. Three photographs. Dim, a bit blurry, but the participants nevertheless recognizable as a tall, dark-haired man leaning on the shed wall while the US Senate's wealthiest representative knelt in damp leaves and breathed ferociously through his nose.

Lamm stopped by the souvenir shop next to the Hilton. For £1.80, he purchased a blue laundry marker and a postcard with an envelope. A postcard (manufactured near Shanghai) of the giant Ferris wheel at South Bank – bone white, four storeys high, impassively hollow against the grey London sky – that he promptly dropped in a rubbish bin. In Kensington Gardens, Lamm sat amid the knee-high grass. He marked the envelope:

ATTENTION: SENATOR RICHARD WESSON.

Taking care not to leave fingerprints, Lamm slid one of the incriminating photographs face-down into the envelope. On the back of the photo, he wrote in a thin, uneven slant deliberately unlike his own.

SENATOR,

I HAVE MORE PHOTOS. GIVE ME WHAT I WANT.

Lamm paused. *What do you want?*

A way out.

A passport.

Therefore, you need cash. But how do you get it?

If you demand that he leaves a million dollars in the park, or in a rubbish bin, or in a phone box, then you're dead. His guards will catch you at gunpoint.

Tell him to deposit the money into your account.

Then he'll know your identity.

Tell him to register a new bank account, so you can withdraw the money.

But to withdraw cash, you need a bankcard.

Tell him to wire you the money.

But to what address?

Was your identity caught by a surveillance camera?

Have the police identified you?

Lamm lay in the grass, thinking.

What you need is an intermediary. Someone you know intimately, who can collect the money. Someone who wants to rattle the senator, who knows how the old warhorse thinks and hates him for it.

No limousine parked outside the penthouse. Lamm pushed the intercom button inlayed with polished walnut burl. She answered drowsily.

'Who is it?'

'Me.'

The pause. She wonders why you're here now.

'You're alone?'

'Yeah.'

Lamm lifted his finger off the talk button. She's calculating the risk? Or she's too drunk, too tired from what she did or didn't do today, to push the buzzer that opens the door.

The snap of the lock. Walking to the elevator, he looked at the marble floor. Hooded, face concealed from the CCTV camera in the lobby.

You heard her via the intercom. She *is* exhausted, though not from a night of fashionable excess, nor sleeplessness induced by indigestion after the Minotaur made her eat the £35 bowl of glorified macaroni last night at The Ivy. No, the creases bordering her eyes are the shock, the unwelcome prick of responsibility, recollection, reality that stepped out of the US Embassy limousine on Park Lane yesterday afternoon. The trauma – that, and the suicidal memories – revived by talking to, listening to, *justifying* herself to the famous silver statue who begot her, yet who remains as foreign as Easter Island's monoliths bearing his emotionless likeness.

Does she know his secret?

Surely she's suspected it.

Lamm recalled Kelly describing her father's weekly relaxation: drinking beer on the back porch with his divorced Washington buddies. *Now you can see it:* the unmasked physicality of those preened, powerful men at the Minotaur's palace, his Satyricon, talking, touching, teasing each other! The Pentagon's closet-lurkers, the gay armchair generals who decant their sexual frustration into military aggression. Everything comes from something.

And Lamm remembered something else. In bed an afternoon ago, after they finished yet before he had to leave, Kelly switched TV channels. They watched an Ultimate Fighting match on ESPN. An inelegant combination of boxing, kickboxing and wrestling, where greased thugs beat the shit out of each other for four-figure sums and fifteen minutes of infamy. Usually the fights degenerate into one three-hundred-pound hulk spread-eagled atop his opponent, holding him down for the count.

'*Ten, nine, eight, seven, six . . .*'

Circling like a toothless shark, the ref counts the numbers. A rippled greased fighter slams the other, pelvis first, into the floor.

Kelly cackled her drunken hyena laugh at the homoerotic theatricality of it all.

'Look at these tough guys climbing all over each other! They love it! They should get a hotel room and fuck!'

She was puzzled that somebody – presumably her father – had paid to watch this fight on pay-per-view. Soon she'll understand.

They sat on the lounge suite. Kelly massaging his right

palm with the tip of her index finger. Concentric circles spiralling slowly, turning him on.

'I'm in trouble with the law.'

She knows, you fool. You're surely not the first fugitive she's taken in.

Lamm glanced at the coffee table. Malik Massawi's obituary on page three of the *Telegraph*.

'I need a passport.'

She withdrew her finger. You've entered a foreign land. The pathetic, penniless place she's been taught to despise all her life.

'Honestly, I don't have a lot of money'

'Your father does. I've got something he wants.'

She looked intrigued, hungry. Of course she'd dug around, but never got any dirt on her old man.

Kelly's mobile started beeping. The alarm she set, in case they fell asleep naked, exhausted.

'He'll be back here soon.'

Lamm started to get up, yet paused. Another lapse of reason. *You shouldn't have mentioned the money.* Lips close enough to touch hers, but he didn't attempt a kiss. Merely felt Kelly's breath, the shallow warm exculpations of a creature externally so perfect, inwardly flawed, maddeningly compelling. This girl born to *everything*, who resurrected herself through sadism, who scavenged him in the park like a hunk of carrion, who knows self-inflicted cruelty the way people know their favourite food. His tongue inches from hers, he whispered into her chaos, her being.

'*Do you want to terrify your father?*'

The twitch of her smile told him what he needed to know.

The TV flashed onto the CNN news. Apart from an

update on the London riots, the bulletin's three minutes concerned the funeral of Pope John Paul II. Lamm and Kelly watched the mile-long procession of pilgrims entering the Vatican. Four million people had already visited the interred Polish pontiff, who succumbed to influenza and Parkinson's disease as famously as the USSR crumbled into history's compost heap. *That*, the CNN anchorman opined, was the Pope's greatest triumph: the dissolution of the communist fairytale that had reduced Poland to scorched earth and empty supermarket shelves.

The funeral was the largest-ever gathering of world leaders and the most watched television event ever. The kings, queens, princes, presidents and prime ministers wore black and pretended to mourn. Gathered not because they especially cared for the grey corpse in white silk, but because their fellow lords of the motorcade – autocrat, theocrat, kleptocrat, democrat – were there too. Clinton the ageless smart-alec schoolboy, compulsively campaigning for his legacy, while Bush the Younger wore his simian scowl of resolve, deaf fortitude, dead certainty. A few feet away stood Chirac, affecting the hook-nosed de Gaullian profile of admonition, arrogance, antipathy that endeared him to his countrymen even before he and Old Europe's other obstinate doorstop, Chancellor Schroeder of Germany, insisted on antiquated notions like prudence, forethought and the rest of the Saddam-appeasing hootenanny that drove Senator Richard Wesson nuts. Must be awkward; the American commander-in-chief sitting alongside those European nay-sayers who pooh-poohed the Iraqi adventure conceived by Reagan's fossilized cheerleaders and a roomful of monkeys banging on typewriters in the Pentagon.

In another row, the Prince of Wales, who'd postponed

his wedding for this funeral to end all funerals, sat stiff as an Oxford oak a few seats from Mugabe the anti-colonialist despot. Moshe Katsav, the president of Israel, hunched two seats away from President Khatami of Iran. Lamm recognized most of the dignitaries; he'd been reading the newspapers cover-to-cover for four days straight. This gathering of heads of state, announced the anchorman, eclipsed even the hallowed throng at Winston Churchill's state funeral back in 1965.

'That's your father's type of funeral.'

'He'll be buried at Arlington with a twenty-one-gun salute. It's what he expects.'

'That's what he deserves? For starting this war and killing half a million Iraqis?'

'You don't get it.' Kelly smiled half-mockingly at the fugitive. 'It's what *America* deserves. We have our kings and queens too.'

A familiar-sounding engine purred in the street. The US embassy limo.

'Have you guessed his secret?'

Before Kelly could answer – her affirmation or the lie that she hadn't – Lamm dropped the envelope onto the coffee table. It landed face up: ATTENTION: SENATOR RICHARD WESSON in black letters.

'I need a hundred thousand dollars tomorrow. That's nothing to him.'

They kissed. Lamm's tongue grazing the soft rim of Kelly's gums, the bevelled edge of her front incisors slightly chipped from when she used to jack open syringes with her teeth. He stood motionless, exhaling into her. Desire stirred, never long dormant, the thirst – for disorder, decrepitude, vengeance, chaos – that bound them together ever since he grabbed her disobedient dog in a neglected grove of Hyde Park.

'Please talk to your father. I'll call you tonight at ten.'

She doesn't reply, like your ghosts.

But look at her: she's intrigued by the intersection of her revenge and your necessity.

The wrecking ball is in that envelope. She'll demolish him. Demolish the father who, through his professional neglect, passively tore her apart in a silent Georgetown mansion where every afternoon she'd stared in vain at his gun, waiting for somebody to tell her *not* to kill herself. The father who betrayed and banished her mother to Europe, who approved the cluster bombs that obliterated the legs of those Iraqi children appearing on the BBC news and in Kelly's nightmares. The father who forced her into the National Guard to be reassembled, limb by limb, into what she hated. Into him.

The razor look she's giving you. Too proud to ask what's inside.

He glanced at the video screen by the door. The Minotaur was walking into the lobby. Lamm ran down the fire escape and escaped into Park Lane.

TWENTY-TWO

Hyde Park. The classic locale for demonstrations ever since the 1830s: the Chartists, the Reform League, the Suffragettes, the Vietnam War protests, the Stop the War Coalition. Commencing midday on Sunday 10 April 2005, another enormous rally was set for the park: the London Against Racism march. A communal demonstration of solidarity against the East End riots, organized by the British Muslim Forum, the National Union of Students and the Love Music Hate Racism alliance. Underneath the barbeque, Lamm awoke to the din of nearly twenty-three thousand protesters ten minutes away on the lawn.

Shouts, chants, horns, sirens and a voice that Lamm recognized, booming through the PA system half a mile away. In its gruff mix of East End slang and Urdu-accented English, the voice thundered in mourning, defiance, dissent.

'*We will not accept violence against my son and other innocent Muslims! We will not accept this injustice! I call on Mr Blair to prosecute the racists responsible for my son's death and the riot. I call on Mr Blair to stop his murderous war against Muslims in the Middle East!*'

The orator was Malik Massawi's father, whose doggedly resilient voice was familiar to the culprit from radio bulletins.

Overhead, the unnerving shudder of news helicopters, their cacophony pricking the hairs on Lamm's skin. This was London's biggest demonstration since the futile antiwar protest on a Saturday in February 2003. Face down in the blanket he'd pilfered from Kelly's wardrobe, Lamm predicted the nearby scene: a vast assembly of British Muslims, of Christian, Hindu and secular protesters too, of firebrand students, curious local residents, police, journalists, TV crews. The crowds there to applaud the rhetoric, to enjoy the free rock concert, to admonish the prime minister who had taken British-Islamic relations to their lowest ebb since 9/11.

They're protesting against you.

Office workers, punks, Old Labourites, pensioners, radical students hoisting banners, Pakistani youths brandishing the teenage martyr's head torn from the *Sun's* front page and stuck on a square of cardboard. Pedestrians yelling their support or their opposition, or just there for the spectacle. On the lawn's northern flank, a stage would soon feature Madness, the Libertines and Billy Bragg. Onstage, alongside George Galloway and the usual celebrities nodding like hungry pelicans, Malik Massawi's father commandeered the fury of twenty-three thousand people. An impassioned performance from this short, moustached man from Kandahar, whose usual audience was the uninterested passenger in the back seat of his cab.

'*Prime Minister, do not ignore us! The East End is burning for the first time in sixty years. London's racist majority killed my son. London's racist majority started the riot! And we, the Muslims of Britain, say enough is enough!*'

The tsunami of applause. Cheering of a conviction

not often heard outside football stadiums and public executions.

From the growing crowd rumbled thunderous chants.

'*The people, united, will never be defeated!*'

'*No to racism! No to Blair! No to racism! No to Blair!*'

Following the concert, the protest would snake down Oxford Street. Already four hundred constables, some on horseback, others clad in helmets and body armour behind perspex shields, manned the pavement up to the junction of Tottenham Court Road. Most of the big Oxford Street stores were closed for the day. Some had boarded their windows with plywood.

Exhausted, excoriated Lamm! He sank into the blankets. The previous night's sleeplessness, the stale air underground; it made a powerful sedative. Last night the restlessness wrought large in his dreams. He was floating; floating out of the barbeque, through the moist teary fronds of the weeping willow, above the silvery moonlit lawns and over London's bejewelled midnight grid, faster, higher, higher, his body a jet until instantaneously he crossed the Atlantic. Hijacked by memory, he flew over New York, experiencing the scene that four years ago he had imagined daily: the steel sequoia forest of Manhattan, growing terrifyingly in the passenger windows as the two airliners commenced their suicide spirals. No destruction there for Lamm; he flew down, down, down between the towers, into the East River where he sank beneath the clear waves of his childhood holidays on Jan Juc beach. Deep in that frigid moat, Lamm felt his fingers through the warm sand of Bass Strait in summertime, searching for cockles, cuttlefish, tiny hermit crabs with pincers like his mother's tweezers. Underwater, meet your ghosts: your grandfather, your mother, Mr Lewski, Rachel Samuels, Malik Massawi. Waiting, watching you in the aqueous endless ether of your memory, your nothingness, your wondering, your life. *Come back!* But the ghosts never say a word.

Again something was pulling Lamm out of the water. But not Scott Greer's strong hands, the hands that accepted an award for bravery from the mayor of New York. These hands were sounds; the stark rattle of a truncheon bashing on the barbeque grate.

You're drowning!

Lamm lurched up, trying to swim, hitting his head on the limestone wall.

More banging.

'Constable, there's a grate. Look!'

Not a metre away, the voice. Terrifyingly calm, relentless.

They've found you.

TWENTY-THREE

No more than fifteen seconds between the commencement of the noise and Lamm grabbing the gun he had stolen from Kelly's wardrobe, yet it seemed like a day at the edge of the abyss. The abyss of your bottomlessness, the *bottomlessness* of your bottomlessness, unmasked and fatal.

This is your Hitler's bunker.

Lamm loaded the gun. Push it in and click; easy. No wonder that America's geeks are murdering their classmates at junior high. Now raise the barrel and shoot yourself between the eyes. Or in the back of the neck, the way George kills Lennie in the dying pages of *Of Mice and Men*.

Mr Lewski! Your ghostly teacher who taught you Steinbeck, looking his students in the eyes, daring you to think! To criticize, to understand, to read a book *an-a-lytically*, as he would say. You never realized how you missed him. Now you'll be together, wherever he is or isn't.

The metal grate wrenched open. Sunlight spilt into the hole. They saw the fugitive's feet.

'There's a man in there!'

Do it!

Now!

Lamm clicked the safety off. This *is* how George kills

Lennie, in the split-second before the inevitable. The final moment before Curly and the ranch hands close in. Choose your defiant death, like the fearless Jews at Masada that your grandmother taught you about. They wouldn't surrender to the Romans.

Do it!

Lamm saw his father in the checkout line at a supermarket in Caulfield, getting scolded by Schiff the plastic surgeon.

Your boy hates everything we love. The boy loves to hate.

That's what he loves. The hatred.

And staring into the ageless remembered universe of Mr Lewski's eyes, Rachel's eyes, Malik Massawi's eyes, George and Lennie's eyes, his mother's eyes, his own eyes, Lamm couldn't do it. Couldn't pull the trigger, any more than Kelly Wesson could when she spent every afternoon staring at the gun she stole from beneath her father's bed in a Georgetown mansion. To endure, you have to live.

A voice outside. Half-man, half-robot.

'Metropolitan Police! Come out with your hands in the air!'

Hands pulling at his ankles. They'll drag you out and skin you like a snake.

'Get the bastard out!'

That familiar voice. Its razor Texan Rs mashed into the anglified burr of verdant Connecticut. No hint of the camp, the queer, the cock-hungry. Here was the Minotaur's macho American oratory, the voice of the eagle on the presidential seal if that bird acquired the power of human speech.

'That's him! The thief!'

Lamm left the gun in the charcoal dust. Live ammo

with the safety off, next to the juice bottle of his urine. The senator will get a shock when he recognizes that gun. Might want to change his sheets too.

'You're certain that's him, sir?'

Three unarmed policemen wearing knife-proof vests, rainjackets, bobby helmets. Handcuffs bit Lamm's wrists. He saw his own painting of the fox fleeing the hunting party, scarlet haemorrhages of terror in the animal's eyes.

'That's the kid who mugged me.'

The silver hair, the pink bull skin, the hard blue eyes drinking you in. *You photographed me last night.* The senator removed his herringbone jacket. He crouched, took a peek, then crawled halfway into the hovel.

'Sir, we'll do that. It's filthy down there!'

'No, I'll take a look myself.'

There she is. At the mouth of the overgrown path, Kelly watched the arrest. Hair unbraided, wearing the black jeans and tan sweater that he tore off her in bed. Usually she never wore the same outfit in a week. No eyeliner, no blush. Her cheeks washed clean by a splash of water or tears. She gazed at Lamm, motionless, as the three constables wondered why an important man like the senator would scramble about in a bum cave.

The Minotaur had threatened to cut her off? But he's not so stupid. He doesn't need a family bunfight in the newspapers. Lamm watched Kelly watching him. Her pale barbed face, obscenely pretty for the maelstrom beneath. The living apology welling in her eyes.

I'm saving him because I need to.

Because I want to.

Underneath the barbeque, her father searched for his future.

'There's no wallet down here. It's trash.'

Strewn in the long grass, these were the things the senator threw out of the hole: a mohair blanket from his own apartment; empty packets of nuts, biscuits, batteries; a juice bottle of urine wrapped in the *Daily Telegraph*. On the front page: POLICE MANHUNT FOR RACIST RIOT KILLER.

Only Lamm noticed the subtle rectangular protuberance in the senator's trouser pocket, the size and shape of the photographs in their paper sleeve.

And the Minotaur looked at Lamm. Enormously relieved, pleased with himself, but grudging admiration in there too. *You fucked my daughter, you stole my gun, you photographed my recklessness, you tried to blackmail me. You would have destroyed me.* A vulnerable glance from this old Washington hand at the subtle crimes of deception, subterfuge, statecraft, who'd learnt his lessons from Henry Kissinger and Roy Cohn when he was a fresh-faced intern at a Manhattan law firm in 1966. A disgraced tennis player – not the Syrians, the Iranians, the Clintons or Ralph Nader – had come closest to destroying Richard Wesson, the senator who might bear the secret of the scabs on his knees all the way to the Oval Office.

'That's the kid who robbed me. Take him in.'

TWENTY-FOUR

The constables led Lamm to the car. *They don't know who you are.*

He looked back at the path. Kelly was gone.

She won't stay. Not now.

He'll take her back to Washington. Back to the mansion on Massachusetts Avenue, to the ten thousand dollar a table galas, to add her sultry presence to meet and greets with the fat cats who finance American royalty. The Minotaur will shake hands and prosper, his war chest will fatten with gifts from big oil, tobacco and pharma, and he'll take a shot at the nomination. Because he found the photographs in your barbeque. You thought that was the safest place! JFK was torpedoed in the Pacific, Reagan took a bullet from Jodie Foster's stalker, but Richard Wesson came close to something worse: his ignominious booting from the closet as the American people see Billy Graham's favourite senator on his knees at 3 a.m. in Hyde Park. The Minotaur's living death as an international laughing stock – even *worse* than your disgrace – was averted by the daughter whom he has, for twenty-one years, tethered like a prizewinning poodle.

Lamm wanted her *now*. To grab her scarred hands, her exquisite gazelle neck, to swallow her lips and scream the truth into Kelly's insides.

You weren't just saving him. You were saving yourself.
You are your father.

Kelly won't destroy her destroyer; she *is* what she is. The war with the warmonger defines her. The hostility, the tension, the thirst to prove her father wrong; it's her soul, her fuel. She needs him as much as she hates him. *That's* what she loves. The hatred.

You saw her tears. The betrayal, the cold resignation. She had changed. You were a fool, intoxicated by her flesh. A desperate, infatuated fool. One of millions.

The policemen pushed Lamm into the patrol car, locking the cuffs onto a grate separating the front seats from the rear. In the belly of the whale.

The ginger-haired constable – Griffith, according to his nametag – yelled into his radio.

'Disturbance at Alpha Bravo. Received. We're on the way.'

Griffith grimaced at the other policemen. 'Bad news. They want backup.'

Up Bayswater Road, the car blazed its sirens through the bottleneck, veered right at Marble Arch and cleaved a throng of two thousand protestors marching to the rally. Lamm noticed the latest edition of the *Sun* folded behind the gear stick. Its front page headline: ARAB SUSPECT ARRESTED FOR RIOT MURDER. Beneath those crimson words, there appeared a skinny, sick-looking boy of about fifteen, wearing a hooded tracksuit, staring into the lens at a police station, clearly terrified. The boy was light-skinned – that is, light-skinned enough to be the culprit in the CCTV video – but unmistakably of Middle Eastern ethnicity. Their antidote to the poison. Lamm read the smaller accompanying headline.

PRIME MINISTER: ARREST PROVES
THAT RIOT MURDER WAS NOT
RACIALLY MOTIVATED

Whatever was happening around the corner, it was louder. Shouts, shrieks, screams. Cheap jagged bells of broken glass.

Griffith barked into the radio. 'We've got a brawl a block west from Marble Arch. Reinforcement needed *now!*'

The constables prepared to leave the car, fastening their helmets and body armour, gripping truncheons. As they unlocked the doors, the crowd surged. About a hundred youths – white *and* black – pelted the sedan with stones, bottles, cans, their feet and fists.

'Send backup! We're being attacked!' Griffith screamed into the radio handset.

At Marble Arch, five police cars couldn't get through. Their sirens blared, but thousands of protestors wouldn't – couldn't – clear a passage. Park Lane's residents watched aghast from their penthouse balconies. Kids smashing the frontage of a Ferrari dealership, chairs hurled through the windows of a svelte café, overturned rubbish bins blocking traffic, ripped garbage bags spilling their rancid guts amid the papery smoke of recycling bins set on fire.

The protestors' chant boomed in unison: *'The people, united, will never be defeated!'*

A riot. Disorder for disorder's sake, the metamorphosis of infectious rage into this polyheaded hydra of destruction, multiplying faster than bacteria as thousands of people vented their anger at Blair, Bush, Britain, Iraq, Malik Massawi's murder, the shameless wealth of Park Lane, the jobs and universities closed to people like them who never scored top marks at a top school, their own precarious employment as cleaners or kitchen hands on the minimum wage; *everything*. Dozens of youths gleefully attacked the police car, rocking it, trying to turn it over, gurning menacingly through the windscreen at the terrified constables.

Griffith screamed into the radio. '*Fucking send backup now!*'

A decorative garden rock smashed a fist-sized hole in the rear windscreen. The policemen lowered their windows a crack, unleashing capsicum spray at the rioters. But the foul mist didn't exit the car, instead wafting inside the cabin. Within a second, Lamm and the three policemen started to choke, their eyes burning like chilli paste was rubbed onto their pupils.

Lamm shut his eyes, breathing hot daggers down his throat. So this is the experience of a gas attack, like when Saddam gassed the Kurds at Halabja. It's an 8.0 earthquake too. The police car's right wheels left the asphalt as nine protestors heaved their collective weight against the chassis. Two hooded boys hurled a steel fence pole at the windscreen, its crystallized web spitting glass fragments onto Lamm's cheek. Sirens screamed, the gilded avenue bursting with horns, shouts, squeals, a man on a megaphone telling the protestors to attack the pigs, while a policeman's robotic voice threatened tear gas if the crowd didn't move back. The police car rocked past forty-five degrees; amid the flash of photographers' cameras, Lamm watched the street – the rioters, the smashed shop windows, the flashing lights, the drizzling faceless sky – turn topsy-turvy. Topsy-turvy as Jan Juc's waves, the East River's deathly rip, the unrequited hopes of Lamm's disappeared years when his whole earthly sphere was a tennis court, bar mitzvah lessons, Mr Lewski's classroom and Rachel Samuels' promising lips. Topsy-turvy because the police car had tipped over. Upside down, strapped into their seats, Lamm and the policemen choked for air.

The people, united, will never be defeated!
Fuck the police! Fuck the police! Fuck the police!

The excruciating din as fence posts battered the car's upturned belly. A white teenager, wearing a balaclava and a Chelsea football jersey, happily smashed the headlights' Perspex shell.

Finally the crowd cleaved as police surged in on horseback. Screams as truncheons and hooves battered bodies in every direction. But a volley of projectiles caught the officers off-guard. A mounted constable felt the brunt of a glass bottle striking his helmet, shattering shards over the horse's sodden mane. Concussed, the policeman tugged the reins and the horse reared, kicking an Indian protester in the back. Lamm watched the spooked mare raise its hind legs, its violin-bow tail thrashing, and stomp a hoof upon the protester's head. Unmistakably a fatality. The victim still gripped his cardboard sign, showing Malik Massawi's coffin cut out from a newspaper pictorial. Written below in red paint: NEVER AGAIN.

Fuck the police! Fuck the police! Fuck the police!

The chanting swelled deafeningly. Rocks, bottles and a few Molotov cocktails hurtled at a riot van. The TV crews sheltered at its flank, four intrepid cameramen breathlessly filming the nation's headline news.

In front of the cameras, a Pakistani teenager approached the upturned police car. The newspapers later revealed that he was Malik Massawi's cousin who had helped to organize the first demonstration earlier that week.

'The people, united, will never be defeated!'

Holding a homemade sign proclaiming NO RACISM NO WAR, his face wrapped in a *keffiyeh* scarf to keep out the gas, Malik Massawi's cousin reached through the car window and gripped Lamm's handcuffed hand.

Feverishly, the cameramen and photographers shot the front-page picture. This fearless young protestor embraces his captured comrade!

'The people, united, will never be defeated!'

As the policemen unleashed their batons, the furious chorus yelled louder.

His right hand grabbed in triumph by Malik Massawi's cousin, his throat stinging from the gas, eyes dazzled by flashing cameras, Lamm began to laugh.

Acknowledgements

I wish to thank the literary agents Donica Bettanin and Jenny Darling in Melbourne and Piers Russell-Cobb in London; Madonna Duffy, John Hunter, Christina Pagliaro and everyone at UQP; James Gurbutt and Sarah Castleton at Constable & Robinson; and Leon Turnbull, John Safran and Bram Presser for their insightful comments on the manuscript in progress.